*Realms Of The Fae 5
Imprisoned By Iron*

Realms Of The Fae 5
Imprisoned By Iron

Avril Sabine

Cracked Acorn Productions
Australia

Realms Of The Fae 5: Imprisoned By Iron

Published by

Cracked Acorn Productions

PO Box 1365

Gympie, Queensland 4570

Australia

978-1-925617-90-0 (Kindle)

978-1-925617-91-7 (EPUB)

978-1-925617-92-4 (Print)

Genre: Young Adult Urban Fantasy

Cover design by Caitlyn Petersen

For the teachers and librarians in my past who encouraged the dreams of a child. And for the ones I know now, encouraging the dreams of other children.

When Audrey and her family become lost on a rural road, they end up with more problems than just car troubles. Kidnappers, an imprisoned knight and Fae who are rapidly losing their sanity, but not their magic. Audrey doesn't know if she'll survive let alone save those she cares about.

*

This story was written by an Australian author using Australian spelling.

Name Pronunciation

Like many names there is more than one way to pronounce the following ones. These are the pronunciations used in this story.

Betsan (bet–san)

Gower (gow–er)

Idris (id–ris)

Luw (lou)

Madlen (mad–len)

Sayer (say–er)

Siani (sea–arn–ee)

Tanwen (tan–wen)

Chapter One

Lightning filled the car with a flash of light, making Audrey temporarily squeeze her eyes closed against the brightness. She breathed out heavily. So much for sleeping through the trip home. She glared at her younger brother, Jordan, who was asleep, his mouth partly open, his breathing even. How could he sleep through the thunder and lightning? She jumped slightly when lightning forked across the sky again, making her brother's sandy brown hair appear nearly white.

She leaned forward, looking at her parents in the light from the dash, the eerie green glow preferable to the bright streaks of light. "How much longer? It seems to be taking longer than usual."

"The roads are wet," Fred said. "Just because it's stopped raining, doesn't mean they're dry."

"It is longer?" Audrey frowned. "Do the headlights

look dim to you?" Maybe it was the lack of streetlights and traffic on the rural roads.

"They're fading," Fred said. "The battery isn't charging."

"How long until we're home?" Audrey peered through the windscreen, trying to see past the dim light on the bitumen in front of the car.

Joan turned in the seat, casting her face in shadows. "We won't be getting home tonight."

The car filled with a flash of light. Audrey jumped again. The dark scenery outside was momentarily highlighted, a landscape devoid of colour. Even her brown hair lacked its various shades of gold, bronze and copper that were naturally scattered throughout it. "What do you mean we won't get home?" Tomorrow was her seventeenth birthday. Her plans had already been put on hold for a visit to her great-grandma's place. All because they shared a birth date and a name. With how little her mum liked being named after Great-Grandma's sister, she would have thought her mum wouldn't have done the same to one of her kids.

Fred's attention remained on the road ahead and he didn't answer immediately. "We can't keep driving in the dark. Not once the headlights go. That'd be too dangerous."

Audrey sat back to peer out the window on her left. A flash of light forked across the sky, lighting up the landscape and draining it of colour. There was absolutely nothing out there. Only sparsely treed, rocky hills in the distance with bare paddocks stretching back from the road towards them. "We're going to pull up on the side of the road?" What if someone ran into them? There wasn't that much space with a gully running the length of the roadside, only a couple of metres in from the bitumen. The visibility outside was terrible. Not that she'd seen any traffic. It felt like they were the only ones left in the world. A world without colour and only the occasional flash of light.

"We don't have a choice," Fred said.

Joan leaned forward, pointing to the left when lightning lit the sky again. "I see a house over there. Who knows, we might get lucky and they'll have a phone we can use to call for help."

Frowning, Audrey took out her mobile phone and checked the coverage. There was none. Could the night get any worse? She was meant to be meeting up with her friends first thing in the morning. They had the whole day planned. Her gaze focused on the time. Less than two hours until her birthday. Being stuck on the side of the road in an electrical storm wasn't her idea of a great birthday. But she was beginning to think she couldn't expect anything else when it came to her birthday.

Jordan made unintelligible sounds, his noises eventually making sense. "Trying to sleep. Can't you stop talking? What happened to leaving before dark so we'd be home early? Should have known the plans would change. They always do."

Audrey looked at her brother as the night lit up. His eyes were mostly closed and he was yawning, his hand barely covering his mouth. "You might want to wake up for this. It looks like we're going to be stranded out here." She thought of the empty esky in the boot of the car. The one they'd packed early that morning with food to have while they were out. "Stuck on the side of a deserted road with no food and very little water."

"We're what?" Jordan peered out the window on his right, cupping his hands on either side of his face, the edge of them pressed against the glass. "Where are we?"

Fred slowed further. "Too far from home to keep going."

"It's anyone's guess," Joan said.

Audrey looked from her mum to her dad. "What's going on?"

"We're not lost," Fred stated.

Audrey sighed. The night kept getting better by the second. "We're lost?"

Jordan echoed her as the car was again filled with a flash of light. "How can we be lost? We've been out here a million times."

"Eight times." Audrey could remember every single birthday she'd been forced to visit her great-grandmother rather than celebrate how she wanted to celebrate. It was always the Saturday around her birthday. Or on it. Like last year and the year she'd turned eleven.

The crunching sound of the tyres going over the loose rocks of a narrow driveway was drowned out by the crack of thunder, light again filling the sky. Joan grabbed the dash. "Look out."

A figure appeared in front of them, lurching to the side, swallowed by darkness when the lightning display ended.

Fred, who'd slammed on the brakes, hunched over the steering wheel as he peered into the night. "I swear he wasn't there a moment ago. It was like he came out of nowhere."

"People don't just appear out of nowhere." Joan gestured to the side of the driveway. "Pull over. We'll walk the rest of the way."

Fred slowly continued up the driveway. "It has to be a hundred metres away. Maybe more."

"Pull over." Joan gestured towards the side of the driveway again.

"That means we'll have to walk that far again in the morning." Jordan leaned forward to peer between the two front seats as lightning lit up the sky. "The place looks like something out of a horror movie."

"Pull over." Joan's words were terse.

Audrey sighed heavily. They were both right. The lights were too dim to see properly and they couldn't leave the car parked halfway down the long driveway. "The sooner we find a landline, the better." Taking out her phone, she unbuckled her seat belt and swung the car door open.

Joan turned in her seat. "What do you think you're doing?"

"Dealing with the problem." Audrey stepped out of the car, which was barely moving, and turned her flashlight app on to brightest. Closing the door on her mum's demands to get in the car, she strode past it, remaining to the side as she held her phone up so the light fell on the driveway in front of the bonnet. She glanced at the car when she heard the sound of a door opening and closing on the other side.

Jordan joined her, striding across in front of the car

to reach her. "Do you think we'll be stuck out here long?"

Audrey shrugged, the splash of light on the driveway moving with the action.

"You do remember the esky is empty," Jordan said.

"I haven't forgotten." She also hadn't forgotten her mum had told her not to go overboard when she'd helped pack it early that morning.

"We're never home on time," Jordan said.

She answered him with a shrug. There was no point going over things both of them already knew. Occasionally, they did make it home on time. Except for the yearly trek to see their great-grandma. They seemed to return from that later each year.

"Mike reckons they're headed for a divorce." Jordan glanced over his shoulder. "Do you think they are?"

"Mike is an idiot. You need better friends." She flinched when thunder sounded and the night lit up.

"So he's not right?"

She glanced at her brother, taking a second look at him. She was surprised at how worried he seemed. He was eighteen months younger than her and sometimes, like now, she could have believed he was at least five years younger. "Didn't I already tell you Mike's an idiot?"

Jordan chuckled. "Yeah, but he is fun to hang out with."

The comment she'd been about to make, banished when lightning again filled the sky, highlighting the house ahead of them. She tried not to think of her brother's earlier words. The house did look like it belonged in a horror movie. It was two storeys high, made of weather beaten timber with flaking paint and had a high peaked roof. A verandah ran across the front, a couple of the railings broken, and the curtains were drawn, dim light seeping around the edges. "Does your phone have coverage?"

Jordan shook his head. "I checked before." He remained silent for a moment. "They drill us about stranger danger all the time and yet we're about to go knock on that door." He glanced at the car that continued to follow them.

"If we stick together, we should be right." She tried not to focus on his words. Any of his words. Yet they played over in her mind. Horror movies. Stranger danger. What else could they do? It wasn't like they could sit on the side of the road all night. Daylight was hours away. And being late March, the evenings were cool, the temperature dropping further in the early hours of the morning.

"Great-Grandma should visit us in Brisbane like she used to," Jordan said.

"Aunt Patty doesn't like to drive in the city," Audrey said absently. The woman wasn't exactly their aunt. She was the daughter of their great-grandma's sister, the three of them living together on the old farm that mainly consisted of the farmhouse and house yards, the rest of the land having been sold years ago.

Jordan looked up at the house when they stopped in front of it. "Does it feel like someone is watching you?"

She lowered the brightness of her flashlight app, not wanting to flatten the battery. His words made a chill travel down her spine. "Will you shut up? You're wasting your breath. No matter what you say, you're not going to creep me out." Or at least she wasn't about to admit to it.

"I wasn't trying to creep you out." Jordan looked over his shoulder at the sound of two car doors opening and closing.

Audrey turned to watch their parents walk towards them. She faced the light from her phone at the ground. "Find out if they have a cordless phone they can bring to the door."

"I was the one who taught you what to do in an

emergency," Joan said. "You don't need to remind me of anything."

Audrey started to point out that both of them had a tendency to tell them one thing then do another. She closed her mouth, words unspoken. She was tired and wanted to sleep rather than get in an argument.

Joan strode up the three steps leading to the verandah. "Bring the light closer." She knocked sharply on the door.

"What if they're asleep?" Audrey stepped onto the bottom step, not wanting to go any closer to the door. Why had Jordan asked if it felt like the house was watching her? Couldn't he have kept that to himself?

Joan knocked on the door again. "There are lights on."

"That doesn't mean anything," Jordan said softly.

Audrey grinned at her brother, reminded of the amount of times their mum had fallen asleep watching a movie. Before she could comment on the memory, the door swung open.

Chapter Two

A tall, thin woman stood in the doorway, her pale skin almost glowing in the light cast from the candle she held, her long hair equally fair and her eyes an impossibly pale blue.

"I'm sorry to bother you-" Joan began.

"Is it just the four of you?" The woman looked past them to the car parked in front of the house.

"Yeah." Fred held out his hand, stepping forward. "I'm Fred. Just plain Fred. Not short for anything."

Audrey winced at her dad's familiar phrase. How many times had she asked him not to say that? It wasn't at all amusing.

The woman didn't shake his hand. "Come in. No need to stand on the doorstep all night." She took a step back. "I'm Madlen."

Joan remained where she was. "We need to use your phone."

"No phone and no power. Are you coming in or spending the night in your vehicle?" Madlen glanced past them as she spoke the word vehicle, her tone letting them know she didn't think much of it.

"Well…" Joan's voice trailed off.

"No one will get any sleep if we spend the night in the car." Fred finally lowered his hand, glancing at it first as if having forgotten he held it out.

"There's plenty of space," Audrey said. "You and Mum can wind the front seats back. Jordan and I don't need a lot of room. We can use the back seat." Staying in the car had to be preferable to entering a strange house. Even with how cold it would get in the early hours of the morning.

Joan looked Jordan up and down. "Jordie is taller than you, Audrey. He'll take up a lot more room than you."

Jordan took a step towards Audrey. "No I won't. Audrey is right. There's plenty of space in the back seat for the two of us."

Madlen began to close the door. "I will expect you to be on your way at daylight."

Fred held out a hand, preventing her from closing the door. "Wait a minute. The kids don't speak for us. If you've got the room, we'd appreciate somewhere to stay for the night."

"The house has plenty of space. It's only me and my nephew who live here." Madlen held the door wide open. "You can stay upstairs."

Fred entered the house, turning to Audrey and Jordan. "Come on. You didn't have to drive all day after an early start."

Audrey shared a look with Jordan. She could see he had as little idea as her about what to do. She remained close to his side as they entered the house, wanting to tell him if they stayed together, all four of them, they should be okay. But she couldn't exactly say anything in front of Madlen. Insulting the woman when she was letting them stay seemed rude.

Fred made introductions as they entered the house, gesturing to each of them in turn.

Madlen closed the door the moment they were inside, not acknowledging any of the introductions. "Would you like a light supper?"

Joan followed Madlen down the hallway. Lit candles and lanterns were placed on every available surface. "I'm afraid the kids have too many allergies. The main ones are gluten, dairy, fructose and nuts."

"I'll have my nephew check what we have that avoids all those ingredients." Madlen stopped at a doorway that led into a dining room. "If you wish to take a seat, I won't be long."

"We're not hungry." Audrey grinned at her brother when he said the same words, both having spoken at the same time.

Madlen looked them over. "I find that hard to believe."

Audrey repeated her words. She could be starving and she'd say the same. People often didn't understand allergies and there'd been too many times when she'd ended up eating something she'd been assured was fine only to learn the hard way that it wasn't.

"I want to sleep, not eat," Jordan said.

Madlen looked from one to the other before turning to Joan and Fred. "Did you want a light supper before bed?"

Fred started to nod, opening his mouth to speak.

Joan nudged his arm. "Sleep. We all need sleep. Food isn't necessary." She glanced at Audrey and Jordan before giving Fred a pointed look.

He sighed. "Yeah, sleep. That's all we need. If you can show us to somewhere we can stretch out…" His voice trailed off, his gaze momentarily drawn to the dining table. "Sleep would be good. None of us are hungry."

Madlen inclined her head. "I'll send my nephew to show you to your rooms." She gestured towards the dining room, a single candle in the middle of the table, the flickering flame casting very little light. The room was dimly lit compared to the entrance and hallway. "That is if you're certain you're not hungry." She took a step away before facing them again. "Do not wander about my home. I don't appreciate it when people invade my privacy."

Jordan didn't speak until Madlen was out of sight. "Do you think we'd find dead bodies if we wandered around?"

Joan pointed a warning finger at him. "Don't even think it. She was kind enough to take us in. Don't make her regret it."

Before Jordan could speak, a wiry man with hunched shoulders hurried towards them. "Madlen said you're staying the night. Can I get you anything to eat? Or maybe a drink."

"No." Audrey spoke the word more sharply than she'd planned, but she was sick of being offered food. Especially when she couldn't accept it.

"You can stay in the upstairs bedrooms." The nephew started to hurry off, heading towards the front door.

Fred strode after him, stepping in front to hold his hand out. "I'm Fred."

Audrey interrupted before her dad could start his

usual spiel. "How many bedrooms does this place have?"

The nephew led the way, glancing over his shoulder. "Don't stray from the rooms you're shown to. Madlen has a lot of sensitive experiments in progress and any interference with them would set her back years." He headed up the stairs.

"She's a scientist?" Audrey asked.

Reaching the top of the stairs, the nephew turned left. "She is nothing so simple as a scientist." He stopped at a closed door, swinging it open. "A bedroom suited for a couple. The sheets on the bed are fresh. We've had visitors recently."

Audrey shined the light from her phone into the room. "What are we meant to do for light?"

"I thought you were going to bed." The nephew opened two doors that were across the hallway. "You can decide which one of you has which room."

Audrey checked the rooms across the hallway. She could see no difference between them. "Thanks."

"I'll take this one." Jordan slipped past Audrey and dropped onto the single bed set in the middle of the wall opposite the door, lying so his feet hung over the end. "I could sleep for a week."

Audrey looked at each of them. "We're staying? In separate rooms." They were meant to stick together.

"I will bring lanterns back for each room." The nephew hurried away.

Audrey stared after him. "He didn't even tell us his name."

"Maybe nephew is his name." Jordan grinned. "Or Madlen doesn't let him have a name. He seemed more like some employee than family. Or a servant. Possibly even a slave."

Audrey remained in the doorway, looking from her brother to the direction of her room. "We should take the mattresses from our beds and sleep in the same room as Mum and Dad."

Jordan peered up at her from under his arm that rested across his forehead. "You can't be serious. Dad snores. No one would get any sleep except him."

Before Audrey could say anything else, the sound of footsteps had her facing the hallway. The nephew hurried towards her. He carried three unlit lanterns, the handles of them resting over one of his arms, the lanterns in a row, none of them touching the other. When he held his arm out to her, she took two of them. "Thank you." She handed one of the lanterns over to her brother who had joined her in the doorway.

Jordan took the lantern. "Got any matches?"

The nephew took a packet out of a pocket, holding

them out to Jordan. "I have another packet. You can keep these for the night."

Jordan slipped the box into a pocket of his jeans. "Thanks."

The nephew inclined his head before handing the third lantern to Audrey. "The bathroom is at the end of the hallway. Let your parents know." He gestured towards the right.

Audrey watched him hurry away. She kept her voice low. "I think we would have been better off staying in the car."

Jordan shrugged. "So, they're a little weird. It's not like you're perfect." He strode to the bedside cabinet and set the lantern down before lighting it. "Weird doesn't make you evil."

Audrey placed the lanterns on the bedside cabinet for Jordan to light. "It doesn't make you good either." She glanced at the door. "I'll give this to Mum and Dad."

Joan answered the door when Audrey knocked. "Is that for us?" She nodded towards the lantern.

Audrey handed it over. "What if we can't ring anyone in the morning?"

"It won't matter. We won't need headlights during the day. There should be enough charge in the battery to get it started, otherwise, we'll push start the car."

"So we just have to get through the night?"

Joan glanced up and down the hallway. "Hush, Audrey. Madlen was nice enough to take us in. Don't go insulting her like that."

She opened her mouth to demand if Madlen was her mum's new best friend. She closed her mouth, words unspoken. She was too tired to get into an argument.

"Say it, then. Whatever you're about to say, spit it out."

"It wasn't important."

"Audrey." There was a warning note to Joan's tone.

She barely managed not to sigh. She was too tired for an argument. She was even less interested in being interrogated. "Is there any food in the car? I'm hungry."

"You know perfectly well if there was food in the car, we'd give you some. Your father and I will have nothing to eat until you two can eat as well. It's too dangerous when we have no way of obtaining medical help if you have an allergic reaction."

This time Audrey did sigh. "Should we sleep in your room?"

"Don't be silly. You're not toddlers any more."

Even though she would have preferred to argue, Audrey managed to keep her mouth closed. As well as the words unspoken. "Goodnight." She strode to Jordan's room before her mum finished saying the words back to her.

"Don't be up all night," Joan called out before stepping into the bedroom and closing the door.

Audrey faced her brother. "This is utter madness."

Jordan was once again stretched out on the bed, his feet hanging over the end and his sneakers still on. "Go to sleep. Aren't you tired?"

She slowly shook her head. She might be tired, but she was more worried about staying in some strange place than getting to sleep. "It doesn't matter. I doubt I could sleep anyway." When her brother didn't comment, his eyes remaining closed, she collected her lantern and strode from the room. Entering the bedroom, she closed the door, placing the lantern on the bedside cabinet before she sat on the edge of the bed. She was tired and exhausted, yet she couldn't stop thinking of all the things that might go wrong. She had no idea how long she sat there before a knock on the door brought her to her feet.

Chapter Three

When she opened the door, the nephew held out a plate of toffee. "Sugar and water. Nothing else."

"No thanks." Besides the fact she wasn't much into sweet food, she didn't know him enough to trust how careful he was with food preparation. What if the toffee was contaminated by one of the things she was allergic to? She liked being able to breathe too much to risk it for a couple of toffees.

"Your family was happy to accept the toffee."

She took the plate of toffee in an effort to keep him quiet on the subject. "Thanks." They'd probably done the same thing. Taken the plate in an effort to get him to leave them alone.

He inclined his head before hurrying away. She watched until he was out of sight before closing the door and setting the sweets on the bedside cabinet next to the lantern. She turned the lantern down as low as possible without putting it out and kicked off her sneakers before she lay on top of the bed linen. As she'd assumed, sleep was miles away. She tossed and turned on the bed, trying to get comfortable. It didn't help.

She didn't know if the bed was too hard or too soft. All she knew was that it wasn't hers. Checking the time on her phone, she momentarily closed her eyes, groaning. It was one o'clock in the morning. Happy birthday to her. She'd be glad when she could stop making these yearly trips on her birthday. She didn't mind visiting her great-grandma, Great-Aunt Joan and Aunt Patty. What she did mind was that the visits always interrupted her birthday celebrations.

Unable to remain in the bed a moment longer, she decided to use the bathroom, slipping her feet back into her sneakers. Leaving the lantern behind, she used her phone to light the way. She was partway back to her room, the bathroom having been as neat and tidy as everywhere else, when she heard a noise downstairs. She tried to ignore it. Tried to return to the room and focus on going to sleep. It was impossible.

She stepped lightly, pausing at the top of the stairs to peer down them. Candles and lanterns were still scattered throughout the area, the lanterns turned down low and some of the candles little more than stubs. Nothing moved. Everything was silent. She found herself creeping down the stairs and making her way through the house. Two hallways later, she heard approaching footsteps and stepped into a nearby room, the interior dark and the door open. Turning off her flashlight app, she slipped her phone into a pocket of her jeans.

Leaning against the wall beside the door she strained to hear who was in the hallway. She smiled as she recognised the nephew's hurried footsteps. He stopped nearby, the sound of his footsteps replaced by a softer, scratchier noise. Swifter, sharper footsteps approached and Audrey wanted to peek around the corner to see who it was.

"Haven't you opened that door yet?" Madlen demanded.

Audrey held her breath, not daring to breathe. Madlen sounded like she was directly outside the room where she hid. What would the woman say if she found her wandering around? Especially since she already sounded angry.

"The key wasn't working," the nephew whined.

"There's nothing wrong with the key. It's your level of competence that is in question."

"It hurts to use it," the nephew complained.

Audrey let out the breath she held, trying to remain as quiet as possible. Would Madlen kick them out if she caught her in here?

"Out of the way." The sound of a door swinging open followed her words. "Make yourself useful and fetch a second bottle. I'll need extra since we have two more to be added to the experiment."

"Not four?" the nephew asked.

"The younger ones will fetch a good price amongst the Fae. You know how much we like the pretty ones." Madlen paused a moment. "Which is why I've never bothered to try and sell you."

Audrey's emotions swung from shock to sympathy and back to shock again. They were involved in human trafficking? She had to get out of here. Had to tell her parents what was happening.

"Why are you still standing there?" Madlen demanded. "Fetch me another bottle." A sharp sound of footsteps sounded in the room across the hallway.

Audrey remained pressed against the wall, listening to the nephew hurry away. Everything was silent, she peered around the edge of the door frame. The hallway was empty. She started to step into it, freezing at the sound of Madlen's laughter.

"You can glare at me all you want, Merrick. Your magic is mine to do what I want with. As are you."

Hearing footsteps hurrying towards her again, Audrey pressed herself back against the wall, holding her breath as she strained to hear what was happening.

"One of the humans has escaped." The nephew was out of breath.

"Then catch them," Madlen said.

"It's a human you gave magic to."

"Then why are you here? Why haven't you caught him?" Madlen demanded.

"He's figured out how to use it. I don't-"

Madlen interrupted him. "Out of the way. Do I have to do everything around here? Where did he go?"

Audrey remained pressed against the wall until she could no longer hear footsteps and no longer hear Madlen's demands. Heart racing, she peered into the hallway. It was empty again. Her gaze was drawn to the open door diagonally across from her. Who was in there? She was halfway across the hallway before she considered that whoever it was might tell Madlen she'd seen them.

It was too late. From the angle his chair was placed on, he could see her. Merrick, Madlen had called him. A soft gasp escaped and Audrey pressed a hand against her mouth, frozen in the hallway. She met his dark gaze, strands of long black hair matted and half obscuring his face. It didn't hide the gag around his mouth, the rag tied tightly. It took her a few more seconds to realise he was tied to the chair, ropes wrapped around his chest and ankles, his hands resting in his lap, tied together.

Audrey took an automatic step forward, tempted to retreat when she caught sight of the look in his eyes. Not that she could blame him. She'd be both angry and crazy with fear if she were the one tied to a chair. The sound of something falling on the floor above her made her jump and she looked between the direction she needed to go to warn her family and the young man tied to the chair. Would she have enough time to set him free and reach her family before Madlen returned?

She took a step away from him, but could go no further. She couldn't leave him behind. No one deserved such treatment. Hurrying forward, she tried not to think about Madlen upstairs with her family. She attempted to remove the gag first. It was impossible. The rag was tied too tightly and it couldn't be undone let alone slipped down. She took a step away from him, planning to go behind him to find the ends of the rope.

Merrick shook his head as he tried to talk past the gag.

"I can't undo it. I'll see if I can undo the rope."

Again he shook his head, nodding in the direction of a workbench along one side of the room. An assortment of tools and items were scattered across it.

She caught sight of a dagger. It had a slightly curved blade and a leather wrapped handle, the guard fancier than an ordinary knife. "That's it? That's what you're trying to tell me? Use the dagger."

He nodded, again trying to speak past the gag.

"Okay. But only the rope. We don't have time for the gag." She picked up the dagger, returning to his side to cut through the ropes. It was easier than she expected. The dagger was a weapon, not something to be found in a kitchen. And it was far more comfortable in her hand than she'd thought it would be.

Merrick plucked the dagger from her, rising to his feet to stagger over to the workbench.

"What do you think you're doing?"

After slicing through the gag, letting it fall to the floor, he picked up a small bottle, holding it out to her. "Taking my magic back."

She stared at the contents. They looked like a silky, dark soil that seemed to contain a dark coloured glitter. "Magic." She slowly shook her head. He'd obviously been held captive too long. "We have to go. My family is upstairs."

"You would risk me being captured again after setting me free?" Merrick demanded.

She took a step away from him at the anger in his voice. "No, but you can't expect me to desert my family."

He stared at her for a moment before inclining his head. "Lead the way."

She took a step towards the door, glancing between him and the exit. "You'll help me?" It seemed too easy.

"As a Fae knight, I have little choice. Where are they before Madlen returns and drains me of what little magic I have left."

It took her a few seconds to start moving, running lightly through the hallways to the stairs and taking every second step to the hallway upstairs. She opened her parents' door first. The lantern was out and her dad snored. Taking out her phone, she turned on the flashlight app, shaking her mum's shoulder.

"That won't help." Merrick returned the nearly empty plate of toffees to the bedside cabinet. "I can only take one of them with us. Which one will it be?"

"They've been drugged?" She didn't wait for him

to answer, racing to her brother's room and opening the door. The lantern was still burning on the bedside cabinet, sitting beside an empty plate. "No." Reaching his side, she shook his shoulder. "Wake up, Jordan. Come on. We have to get out of here." He remained silent, breathing evenly, looking too young. He still wore his sneakers, his feet hanging over the end of the bed. She blinked, realising tears formed. Running the back of her hand across her eyes, she tried once more to wake her brother.

"Is this who you want to take with us?" Merrick entered the room. "You need to be quick." He opened the bottle, pouring the contents into the palm of his hand, holding both the dagger and the small bottle in his other hand.

The words she started to speak vanished like the contents of the bottle vanished into Merrick's skin and she stood staring at him.

Merrick grabbed hold of her arm, shaking her lightly. "Focus. Who do you wish to take with us?"

"Take where?"

"I wish I could say to safety."

"Find him." Madlen's voice rang out in the hallway.

"Too late." Merrick formed an autumn leaf, the air filling with the scent of baked apples. He let the leaf fall to the floor as he grabbed hold of Jordan, dragging him from the bed as he continued to hold Audrey's arm.

Chapter Four

Before she could protest his treatment of her brother, he stepped on the leaf and the world shimmered and went out of focus, coming back into focus as a forest. Drawing her arm from his grip, she slowly backed away from him, shaking her head. "This isn't possible." It was late afternoon and nearby she could hear the sound of a stream as it cascaded over rocks. "You're not real. None of this is real. I ate the toffee, didn't I?"

Merrick lowered Jordan to the ground. "If you did, you'd be sound asleep. Why didn't you eat the toffee when everyone else did?"

"I didn't want to risk it."

"You suspected her of planning something like this?" Merrick gestured towards Jordan.

"No. I have a lot of allergies. I didn't trust her to give me something that was safe to eat." Her gaze was drawn to her brother. "Jordan shouldn't have risked it either."

"I can cure your allergies."

"How?" she demanded.

"Magic." He held out his hand, glittery, coarse soil forming in it. "It will cause other problems though. But you will be able to eat what you want."

Shaking her head, she took another step back from him. "All I want is to get my parents and go home." She glanced at her brother. "Along with Jordan."

The soil sank back into his hand. "I can't return there. Especially not while I'm so weak." Lowering his hand, he took a step towards her. "I can take you to my family's estate and see if someone there can assist you."

"It's my birthday." Her voice was soft and she heard a note of bewilderment in the tone. Which she hadn't expected. "I was to spend the entire day with my friends." She scanned the area. "In the city. In Brisbane. Not in some strange forest with my brother drugged and a stranger telling me he can give me magic. Things like this don't happen in real life. So that means none of this can be real."

"Your logic is flawed." He held out his hand. "I'll see that you and your brother are returned to your home and then we'll be even. Do you accept that as a suitable payment for helping me escape?"

She didn't know what to say. Didn't even know what to think. She again glanced at her brother. She should be checking to see if he was okay. But she was afraid of what she might learn. Then it struck her. She had no idea where she was, no idea if her parents were alive and absolutely no idea if her brother would be okay. Worst of all, she didn't know what Merrick would do and if he was as bad as those she'd rescued him from.

"I would never deliberately hurt you."

She met his dark gaze. Could he read minds? She glanced around, looking for an escape. There were plenty. Numerous directions she could run in. But where would they take her? And what other dangers would she end up in?

"I would sooner hurt my niece than harm you and her, I would die for."

"Niece?" It seemed strange to think of him with a family. With his wild hair and intense gaze, he seemed more like he belonged in this forest than with other people.

He ran his fingers through his hair, pushing it back from his face. "My sister's daughter." His expression hardened. "If something has happened to either of them I will kill those who harmed them."

She froze when she caught a glimpse of his ears. They were slightly pointed, not at all human. "Elf?"

"Fae. You humans are all the same."

It was impossible to miss the disgust in his tone. For a second it made her forget the earlier tone. "You would kill people?" Shock and fear raced through her as his words sank in.

"You act like I'm about to murder someone. Deaths are common in battle and war."

"War." The word escaped from her, causing her to once again scan the area. How could such a peaceful place be at war?

He took a half step towards her. "You do know I won't hurt you, don't you? That I'll protect you." He moved slowly.

She had the impression that he treated her like he would have treated a wild animal, one easily startled. "I want to go home." She felt lost and confused.

"The best I can do for now is take you to my family's estate." He took another step towards her, slowly closing the distance between them. "I wouldn't dare take you to the dark Fae court. Your beauty would put you in danger."

"Beauty?"

He laughed softly. "You were expecting better praise than that?" He gently took hold of her hand.

She shook her head. "My skin is too pale and I burn easily and have too many curves in some areas and not enough in others."

"Perfect." His voice was soft, very little space between the two of them. "Who needs the sun? We dark Fae prefer the nights."

"I.. you…" She shook her head, trying to focus on the current situation rather than be drawn in by the intense look in his eyes and the promises in his voice. "I need to go home." Even to her, the words sounded like they lacked conviction. She tried again. "I need to go home." She tugged her hand from his. "If you truly owe me, take me home. Me and my brother."

"What is your name?" He glanced at Jordan. "You mentioned your brother's name, but not yours." He captured her hand again. "I'm Merrick."

She once more drew her hand out of his grip. "Audrey. Are you going to take me home?"

"I'm afraid I can't. It took too much from me bringing us to my realm."

"Realm?" She cringed at how many times she'd found herself repeating his words today. She sounded like an idiot. But this wasn't a typical day. She should have known it would turn out to be a disaster.

Although, for all she knew her birthday was over. How much time had they lost in travelling here? "What day is it?"

His lips curved into a gentle smile, one that was almost an apology. "You have so much to learn."

Again she drew her hand from his grip. This time she took a step back from him. "What day is it?"

He shrugged. "Time runs differently between the realms."

"Realms?" She almost growled in frustration. She needed to stop repeating his words like a parrot. "Where are we?"

"In the realms of the Fae."

"Where exactly in the world is that? How far is it from Brisbane?"

He didn't answer her straight away. "We aren't in your world anymore. We're in mine."

The words didn't immediately sink in. When they did, they had her heart racing as she backed away from him. "No. Tell me the truth. Where are we?"

A smile fleetingly appeared, this one also apologetic. "I'm Fae. It's impossible for us to lie. Avoid the truth, word things ambiguously, but not lie. Our magic prevents it."

A shudder went through her and she closed her eyes, swaying on her feet. "This is all real?" She opened her eyes when his hands rested on her shoulders.

He met her gaze, his once again intense. "I will protect you. Until I can return you to your home, or see that someone else does, I will protect you."

She tried to say something. Anything to break the tension between them. All she could do was stare into his eyes and wonder why she didn't run. Yet she trusted him. His slightly pointed ears and the power that seemed to surround him should have made her wary of what he planned to do. "I don't need you to protect me." What she needed, as she'd already told him, was for someone to return her to her world. To her home.

He stilled. "Do you reject the offer?"

She started to say yes, the words remaining unspoken at the sense of danger that washed over her. "I don't understand anything." She looked up at him, her gaze clashing with his. He was the only person who could return her home. What if something happened to him and she was stuck here? "I'm scared." The soft words escaped and she wanted to take them back the moment they were spoken.

He lifted his hand from her right shoulder, running it across her cheek and brushing strands of hair back from her face. "I would tell you there's nothing for you to fear, but it would be a lie. All I can do is offer to protect you to the best of my ability. Although you may not think much of my protection when you learn I was supposed to escort my sister and her daughter to my parents for a visit and I have no idea where they are now."

"What happened?"

"There were a dozen of us. Ten of my warriors travelled with us. Four of them were knights. We were ambushed. Normally no one would attack such a heavily armed group of travellers." He held her gaze a moment before glancing away. "It was as if they expected us. Knew when we'd arrive and how many of us there'd be."

"They were kidnapped by Madlen too?"

"I don't know." Again he held her gaze a moment before he spoke. "But I will find out. Which means I need to go to my parents' place to find out if they arrived."

She wanted to protest. What about her parents? Her brother? Herself. "How old are they? Your sister and niece."

"My sister is sixty-eight and her daughter is sixteen."

"Sixty-eight?" The word escaped from her. "She had a kid at fifty-two?"

He laughed softly. "We Fae age differently to you humans."

Shock raced through her. "How old are you?" Surely she hadn't been drooling over an old man.

"Eighteen. I won't be nineteen for another six months. And you? What age did you turn today?"

"Seventeen."

His lips curved into a smile. "A little older than I thought. I'd assumed you sixteen."

The smile made her feel awkward. She glanced away, hoping she didn't blush. "This conversation isn't helping us sort anything out."

"Wait here." He glanced at Jordan. "I need to check something before I take you to my parents' estate."

Chapter Five

When Merrick started to walk away, Audrey grabbed hold of him, not wanting to be deserted. What did she know about forests? She'd been raised in a city. "You're not leaving us alone. Anything could be here."

He captured her hand, removing it from his arm and keeping hold of it. "I need to examine the road where we were ambushed. I don't have the strength to carry your brother around. Not after being held by Madlen for days. Possibly more than a week."

"You don't know how long she had you imprisoned?"

"I was kept in that room. I had no idea if it was day or night or how much time passed." He lightly squeezed her hand. "Stay with your brother. He could wake at any time. You don't want him to wake and find himself alone." He let go of her hand.

She watched him walk away, the trees quickly hiding him. It took all her self-control not to run after him and beg him not to leave them alone. Instead, she forced herself to walk to her brother, crouching at his side. Reaching out a hand, she hesitated. Was Merrick correct? Would he wake soon?

She tentatively placed a hand on his chest. The relief she felt was dizzying and she sat at his side, her legs unable to hold her in a crouch any longer. He was alive. That was a start. She left her hand on his chest, the beat of his heart comforting. She couldn't remember a time he hadn't been in her life.

Her best friend, her worst enemy, the one who drove her crazy and the one who was always there for her. Anger rushed through her. How dare Madlen try to harm him. How dare she try to sell the two of them. Her other hand tightened into a fist, her right hand remaining pressed against her brother's chest. She needed to return to Madlen's house so she could free their parents. Somehow.

A sound behind her had her struggling to her feet, her body tense until she realised it was Merrick. "Did you learn anything?"

"Nothing I didn't already know." He crouched at Jordan's side, checking him over before looking up at her and holding out a hand.

She didn't take it.

He lifted Jordan's hand, still holding out his own. "Hold onto him. It'll make it easier for me to take us to my parents' estate."

She took Jordan's hand from him, crouching beside Jordan, on the opposite of his body to Merrick. When he held out a hand to her again, she took it, meeting his gaze. "I need to rescue my parents."

He inclined his head.

She started to ask him what that meant when the scent of baked apples filled the air, another scent twining through it. A metallic one.

Merrick frowned at the leaf he held, the edges of it curled and blackened. "There's something wrong with my magic."

"Figure it out later. I need to find a way back to Madlen's place so I can rescue my parents."

"I can't use it." Merrick continued to frown at the leaf in his hand.

"You used it to get us here. Why can't you use it now?" Audrey demanded.

He looked up from the autumn leaf and met her gaze. "There was nothing wrong with it before." He frowned at the leaf again. "I don't know what's happened, but something has."

She slowly shook her head. "We're not staying

here." She pulled her hand away from his. "Do you understand? We're not staying here."

"It wouldn't be safe to stay here. The forest is full of wolves of an evening. We need to find somewhere to stay before then." Merrick tucked the leaf into a pocket as he rose to his feet. "Wait here while I scout the area."

She scrambled to her feet. "You are not leaving us behind."

His gaze roamed her face before he spoke. "You don't trust me to return."

"I don't know you." She resisted the urge to apologise at the hurt she saw in his eyes. "You don't know me."

He briefly touched her cheek. "I do." He glanced at her brother before meeting her gaze again. "You're fiercely protective of your own. And loyal." A smile made a brief appearance. "And resilient. You didn't know about Fae before today, did you?"

She shook her head. "Not unless stories count."

He continued to hold her gaze. "I will return. Before dark." He lifted her hand and brought it to his lips.

He was gone before she could say anything. Pressing her hand against her chest, she stared in the direction he'd taken. Fae were real. So was magic.

How many other things, that were supposed to be myths, were real?

"Aude?"

She spun at the sound of her brother's voice, hurrying to his side. "How do you feel?" He sounded terrible and didn't look much better.

"Where are we?" He squinted as he looked around. "How did we get here?"

"You wouldn't believe me." She didn't believe herself. "Can you stand?" She held out a hand to him.

Taking her hand, he struggled to his feet. "I feel odd."

She pressed a hand against his face, trying again when he brushed her hand aside. "You seem to have a temperature." Not that she knew if that was good or bad.

"I didn't say I was sick. Just that I feel odd." Jordan frowned. "Like I'm not quite me. What happened?"

"I don't know." Her words were cautious. "At least not exactly."

"Then how about you tell me what you do know?" He glanced around the area again. "Is there anywhere to sit down around here?"

"I don't know." She was beginning to think there was a lot she didn't know.

He staggered to a fallen tree checking the trunk over before sitting. "What aren't you telling me?"

She stared silently at her brother. Words filled her mind, but she didn't speak a single one. How could she tell him? How could she convince him?

He continued to look up at her. "Aude? What's going on?"

The fear in his voice reminded her of her own. She sat beside him, unable to look in his direction. "You know I wouldn't lie to you. Not when it really counts."

"Where are Mum and Dad?"

She closed her eyes, trying not to think about her last sight of them. "Jordan? You trust me, don't you?" This time she did look in his direction, seeing her own fears reflected back at her from his eyes.

"Yeah. I trust you."

She swallowed, the sound seeming loud. "We never should have got out of the car." She looked at the ground. A scattering of dainty, blue flowers peeked through the grass. "They're still there." She met his gaze. "Mum and Dad. Madlen has them."

"What do you mean 'she has them'?" he demanded.

"I couldn't take them with us. It was the toffee. You weren't meant to eat anything. You know you weren't." Anger rushed through her. "Mum said they wouldn't eat anything." She grabbed his arm, shaking him. "Why? You know better than that."

"I was starving and the nephew said they only had sugar and water in them. It was better than nothing. It felt like my stomach was eating itself."

She tried not to think about how hungry she was. "Better it had eaten itself."

"Where are we?" Jordan asked again.

"Nowhere we've ever heard of before."

"Where?"

Movement caught her attention and she turned to see Merrick slowly walking towards them. She started to rise, wanting to go to him when she saw how exhausted he looked.

Jordan grabbed her arm, keeping his voice low. "Who is that?"

"Madlen had him imprisoned in her house." She held Merrick's gaze as he continued towards them.

He stopped several metres away. "I found a deserted cottage we can stay in. The ground floor isn't secure, but we should be able to barricade the stairwell and be safe upstairs."

"Cottage?" Jordan looked from one to the other. "What is going on?"

She almost laughed at hearing her brother parrot

Merrick's word back at him. She was glad it wasn't only her.

"After we're settled. The day grows late and we don't want to be wandering the forest after dark." Merrick held out a hand to Audrey.

She gave a single shake of her head, helping her brother to his feet, clutching at his arm when he stumbled and staggered forward. She slipped an arm around his waist, supporting him as they followed Merrick.

Jordan draped an arm around Audrey's shoulders, leaning heavily on her. "I feel worse. Like I might be getting sick."

Merrick glanced over his shoulder. "You need to eat. Not human food. Fae food. You'll have to regularly eat it for the rest of your life or you'll sicken and die. Unless you choose to have magic and then you can eat whatever you like."

Jordan laughed. "Yeah, right. Fae food."

"Jordan." She couldn't say more than his name. How was she meant to tell him everything? Especially when she didn't really understand what was going on.

"Why won't you tell me anything?" Jordan demanded.

Merrick again looked over his shoulder. "He will have to know eventually."

She nodded. He did need to know, but she'd rather tell him when she had something good to tell him too. Some hope that they'd be able to survive the situation. Right now, she wasn't certain of anything. Including their chance of survival.

"Aude."

She glanced at Jordan.

"I trust you." His words were soft, spoken only for her.

She drew in a deep breath, wishing she could close her eyes and pretend none of this was happening. "This isn't our world."

"What does that mean?"

She thought of and discarded several answers. "That we're screwed. In a big way."

"Oh." He remained silent a moment. "It's the next day, isn't it? Your birthday."

"I think so." Surely she'd be hungrier than this if she'd missed two days.

"Happy birthday."

"Thanks." She leaned her head against him for a second. "We will get home."

"What about Mum and Dad?"

"We'll find them too," she stated.

"Okay."

They remained silent as they continued to follow Merrick to the cottage. Reaching it, they stood out the front of the dilapidated building. It was nestled amongst the trees, all the windows broken and the front door missing. It was a small building considering it was two storeys high and a vine grew wild over the right hand corner.

"Where the hell are we?" Jordan demanded. He pulled away from Audrey, taking a few unsteady steps towards the building. "I doubt the upstairs of that place can be secured."

"I'll gather wood. It's safe for the two of you to enter the cottage."

Chapter Six

Once again, Audrey found herself staring after Merrick, not having managed to speak before he'd left.

"Are we really staying in there?" Jordan nodded towards the cottage.

"Yeah." It wasn't like they had anywhere else to stay and she didn't want to come face to face with a wolf.

"How are we meant to get home?"

She thought of the leaf Merrick had formed. "I don't know."

"How did we get here?"

"I'll tell you everything later." She headed towards the cottage. Hopefully much later when they weren't stuck in this place and had their parents back. "We should see what's in there."

"I bet it's not food." Jordan ran a hand across his

stomach. "Do you think he was telling the truth about needing to eat Fae food. Whatever that is."

"Yeah."

"What if I'm allergic to it?"

She paused at the gaping door of the cottage to peer inside. "I don't think you will be." If it was magic, then she doubted either of them would be allergic to it. Not from what Merrick had said.

"Are we going in there?"

"Yeah." She remained by the doorway, unable to bring herself to take the first step into the place. The interior was dim, the only light coming in through the broken windows.

"What's wrong?" Jordan remained at her shoulder, peering over it.

She forced herself to enter the decrepit cottage. "Nothing." All further words vanished when she noticed the stairwell in the far corner. It was sandwiched between the outer wall and one that ran up the side where rails would normally be. From where she stood, it looked narrow and dark. She took a step backwards.

Jordan stepped around her. "What are you doing? You nearly stepped on me."

"I can't-" She turned away, ready to flee, running into Merrick who carried an armload of firewood.

"Is something wrong?" Merrick looked upwards. "Is there a wild beast upstairs?"

"We didn't get up there," Jordan said. "I'll go check."

"Audrey?" Merrick placed the firewood on the floor, examining her when she didn't answer.

Her gaze was continually drawn between the stairwell and the exit. How could she walk up that narrow stairwell? She could already feel the walls closing in on her, making it difficult to breathe.

Merrick brushed his hands off on his torn trousers before gripping her shoulders and peering into her eyes. "You're terrified."

She shook her head, unable to look away from his dark eyes.

"Yes, you are." His grip on her shoulders tightened. "What happened?" He glanced past her. "Are you certain there are no others here? No creatures. No people."

"We're alone."

A smile briefly appeared. "Other than your brother." His voice was low and there was humour in his tone.

Her gaze was drawn to his lips when they again briefly curved into a smile. "I can't stay here." The lengthening shadows made the place feel smaller. She dreaded to think how small the stairwell would feel in the lack of light from the ending day.

Jordan came down the stairs, his feet loud against the timber. "There's nothing up there."

Merrick continued to meet Audrey's gaze. "Take the firewood upstairs. The fireplace looked like it should draw well enough."

Audrey waited until she heard her brother heading up the stairs. "I can't go up there."

"You will." He let go of her shoulders to capture one of her hands, tugging her towards the stairs, his other arm around her waist.

"Let me go." She spoke the words through clenched teeth, trying not to give in to the panic that threatened to overwhelm her.

"The wolves will be out shortly, there's something wrong with my magic and the ground floor isn't secure." He stopped at the foot of the stairs, again meeting her gaze. "I said I'd protect you."

"There's-" She broke off when he tossed her over his shoulder. They were partway up the stairs when she was finally able to move. Struggling to escape, she hit at him, her breathing rapid as the walls felt like they were closing in on her. A roaring sound filled her ears.

Jordan called out as they entered the room upstairs.

Audrey had no idea what he said, his words a blur. All she could think of was escape. Her body slid towards the floor and a scream escaped. Before she could land on the wide timber planks, Merrick pressed her against the wall, his body against her, his hands capturing hers as she continued to strike out at him. Her vision was filled with his face.

"You are safe for the moment." Merrick repeated the words several times.

She stilled, her brother's words finally becoming clear. He was demanding her release. Letting out a shuddering breath, she sagged against Merrick, closing her eyes as she tried to rid herself of the image of the walls closing in on her. It was worse with her eyes closed. Opening her eyes, she saw a scratch on his cheek, a thin line of blood forming across it. "Sorry."

"Are you unharmed?" Merrick asked. "Did I hurt you?"

Jordan fell silent, remaining close, warily watching them.

Seeing the worry in Merrick's eyes made her think of his earlier promise. "You didn't hurt me."

"Are you certain?"

She drew in a shuddering breath, nodding. "You can let me go."

He relaxed his grip. "You won't run?"

"I'm thinking of spending the rest of my life in this room." There was no way she was leaving by the stairwell.

Merrick chuckled, a startled sound. "You will leave tomorrow. Either on your feet or on mine." He turned to Jordan, stepping away from Audrey. "Bring up the rest of the firewood."

Jordan didn't move, only glared at Merrick.

"I'll clean out the fireplace." Merrick glanced at the other end of the single room, a stone fireplace dominating the far wall.

"If you ever hurt her–" Jordan broke off, leaving the warning hanging.

Merrick met Jordan's gaze before he spoke. "I would never deliberately hurt Audrey."

"Good." Jordan glanced at his sister before he headed down the stairs.

Audrey followed Merrick to the other end of the room, making a vague gesture towards his cheek. "I really am sorry."

He looked up from the fireplace he crouched in front of. "It will heal. If there wasn't something wrong with my magic, I'd use it on the scratch. It would be gone in seconds."

"How do you know there's something wrong with your magic if you don't use it?"

He returned to cleaning out the fireplace and laying the fire. "The scent of my magic shouldn't change. Nor should the autumn leaf I form to transport myself. It also feels strange. Like it isn't exactly my magic."

Her stomach rumbled and she pressed a hand against it.

Finished with the fireplace, Merrick rose to his feet, dusting his hands off on his trousers. "I saw apple trees not far from here."

"I can't eat them. Along with a lot of other allergies, I have fructose malabsorption."

"What can you eat?"

She shrugged. "Meat, eggs, potatoes, rice." She shrugged again. "There are a lot of foods I can eat." But she doubted any of them would be found nearby.

"If I had a hunting bow, I'd bring down a deer for you." He took out the knife he'd tucked into the side of his boot. "But this is all I have."

Jordan entered the room, dropping the firewood by the doorway, striding towards them. "What is going on?" His gaze frequently went to the dagger.

"I need to shave some wood off for kindling. The

less magic I use to light the fire, the better." Merrick picked up one of the smaller logs.

Jordan slipped a hand into a pocket of his jeans, drawing out a box of matches. "Will these help?"

Nodding, Merrick held up a hand.

Jordan tossed the box to him.

While Jordan stacked the firewood against the wall beside the fireplace, Merrick lit the fire. He then strode to the doorway, pausing by it. "I'll barricade the stairs. Remain up here."

Audrey sat by the fire, the light from it comforting. There was no way she was about to go down those stairs. "I already told you. I plan to live up here for the rest of my life."

Merrick smiled at her before stepping out of sight.

Audrey assumed he went down the stairs, but unlike her brother, she couldn't hear him leaving. He was gone so long that night had completely fallen and she began to worry something had happened to him. When she heard wolves howl in the distance, she sat up, having been leaning against her brother who sat beside her. "Did you hear them?"

Merrick entered the room, shirtless and carrying four saplings bundled under one arm, the branches removed, the base of them snapped off. His shirt was bundled up in his other hand. "I barricaded the bottom of the stairs against them." He set the saplings by the fire and spread out the shirt. "Can you eat carrots?"

"Yes." Jordan leaned forward. "A limited amount, but we can eat some."

Merrick barely glanced at Jordan. "Audrey?"

"We both can." She rested a hand on her brother's arm. "I'm not about to eat and let my brother go hungry."

Merrick gave them three carrots each. "I've washed them in running water so they're safe for you to eat." He glanced at Jordan before returning his attention to Audrey. "Not that it would matter with your brother. He's already eaten Fae food and will sicken further if he doesn't have more."

Audrey took one of the carrots from her brother and handed it and one of hers to Merrick. "I'm not about to let you go hungry either."

Merrick tried to return them to her. "I brought them back for you."

"Did you eat anything while you were gone?"

"I can collect apples in the morning. There are no limits to what I can eat." He set the two carrots back on the shirt. "You can have them for breakfast."

"If we survive the night." Jordan bit into one of the carrots.

Merrick picked up the saplings and retreated to a spot near the door before sitting down and taking the dagger out of his boot.

Chapter Seven

Audrey watched Merrick sharpen the broken end of the sapling into a point as she ate the carrots. They did little to help with her hunger pains. How long would they be stuck in this world? Or realm as Merrick called it.

He looked up from his whittling, meeting her gaze from across the room. His hands stilled.

She looked away, hoping the warmth she felt in her cheeks could be attributed to the fire she sat near rather than the embarrassment she felt at having been caught watching him.

Jordan leaned close. "Should we be panicking?"

Audrey shrugged.

"What about him?" Jordan glanced at Merrick who'd returned to whittling. "We don't know him. How can we trust him?"

She found herself watching him again. The way he

shaved curls of wood from the timber, the muscles in his arms and chest tightening with the action. "I trust him."

Merrick looked up, his hands stilling again as he met her gaze.

She stared back at him, unable to look away this time. Had he heard her? How good was the hearing of a Fae?

A wolf howled. An eerie cry that was echoed by others throughout the forest, seeming to curl around the cottage as if it was surrounded.

Jordan stared at the doorway leading to the stairs. "Think they'll be able to get up here?"

"I hope not."

Merrick returned the dagger to his boot and rose to his feet, leaning the sharpened saplings against the wall except for one. "They'll need to get past me before they can enter."

Audrey found his words surprisingly comforting. Which was ridiculous. He had a handful of sharpened sticks and, from the cries she heard outside, there was easily a dozen wolves out there.

Jordan leaned in close, lowering his voice even further. "He can hear us, can't he."

She met Merrick's gaze, a smile partially forming.

"Does it matter? We're not saying anything he can't hear."

The two of them fell silent, Audrey drifting off to sleep only to be jerked awake at the sound of the wolves closer than they were before.

Merrick looked up from the fire he was adding more wood to. "They haven't entered the cottage yet."

After a glance at her brother, and seeing he was asleep, she kept her voice low. "Do you expect them to enter?"

His gaze roamed her face for a moment before he answered. "There's evidence they've been inside before. Downstairs."

"Then why did we hide in here?" Audrey demanded. "Why didn't we find somewhere safer?"

"There is nowhere safer." Finished with the fire, he rose to his feet and returned to his post by the door.

She stared after him, his shirt still off, his muscles shifting and tensing as he picked up one of the sharpened saplings. Her gaze slowly travelled upwards and she looked away when she realised he watched her. She eventually looked back, surprised to find he continued to watch her, a slight smile curving his lips. "You've brushed your hair." She blurted the words out when she realised his hair was drawn back from his face, the knots gone, a scrap of material tying it at the nape of his neck, a fringe that was long at the sides framing his face. It made his pointed ears noticeable.

"Did you think I was some wild creature?"

"No. Of course not. I just…" Her voice trailed off. "Where did you find a brush?"

"I finger combed it."

"Oh." She felt her cheeks heat and tried to think of a way to change the topic before she ended up looking even more of an idiot.

"If it comes to a fight, I want to be able to see what's coming at me."

"Oh." Again she could think of no reply. It wasn't like she was accustomed to situations like this.

A sound downstairs had him pushing away from the wall and peering into the darkness of the stairwell. "Wait up here."

She scrambled to her feet. "You can't go down there."

"I'm only going partway down to see if the barricade is holding." He stepped out of sight.

She hurried after him, making it as far as the doorway. Freezing, she stared into the darkness, the firelight barely reaching there. "Merrick?" Clasping her hands together, she tried to remain where she was rather than flee to the fireplace. She should be over this by now. Yet she wasn't. Her breath caught in her throat when she heard another sound from below. She fumbled for her phone, wanting to use the flashlight app. The screen remained black.

"Stay upstairs," Merrick said.

She strained to see him, his voice having come from near the bottom of the stairs. "What's down there?"

There was no answer. Slipping her phone into a pocket of her jeans, she remained in the doorway, unable to bring herself to move forward. "Merrick?" Once again, there was no answer.

"Aude? What's going on?"

She turned to face her brother who remained on the floor by the fireplace, rubbing at his eyes. She had no idea what to tell him.

"Aude?"

A sound down below had her facing the doorway again. Like before, she could see nothing. She tried to force herself to take a step forward. Her heart raced and she remained where she was. Her hands curled into fists. This was ridiculous. She was no longer five-years-old.

Jordan joined her in the doorway. "Can you see anything?"

She shook her head, unable to speak. Over and over she mentally berated herself. It made no difference.

Jordan picked up one of the sharpened saplings leaning against the wall. "Should we help him?"

She grabbed her brother's arm, keeping him beside her. She shook her head, her grip tightening on his arm when he tried to pull away. "Don't go down there." The words were little more than a whisper.

"What is-" Jordan broke off when a rumbling growl travelled up the stairwell. He leaned close to Audrey, whispering to her. "Do you think it can get up here?"

"I don't know." She kept her voice as soft as her brother's. "We should move away from the doorway in case it can." There was no way they'd see it coming before it could be upon them if they remained where they were. She grabbed one of the sharpened saplings. There was now only one left against the wall.

Jordan retreated with her and stood at her side by the fire. "How long has he been gone?"

She shrugged. She couldn't even check the time on her phone.

"I'll see-"

Again she grabbed her brother's arm before he could move away from her. "No."

"We can't stand here and hope he returns."

She wished she could say they'd go downstairs and check on Merrick. It would have been a lie. There was no way she could bring herself to travel down those stairs.

"Aude."

She couldn't reply, just continued to hold tightly to his arm.

He tried to shake her off. "Let me go and see. You can wait here."

"No." She wasn't about to let her brother go down there alone. "We don't know if Merrick is downstairs."

"I doubt he'd have left us here," Jordan said.

"That's not what I meant. He might be outside."

Jordan started to speak, his words interrupted by snapping and snarling downstairs. He wrenched his arm from her grip and ran towards the doorway. An extremely large wolf burst into the room, causing Jordan to stumble backwards. When the wolf tried to attack him, he fell, landing sprawled on the floor in an attempt to avoid the attack.

She threw herself between her brother and the wolf, jabbing in the direction of the creature with the sharpened sapling. "Get away from him. Go on." Behind her, she heard her brother struggling to rise.

"Are you crazy?" Jordan came to stand at her side, holding the sharpened sapling ready.

She thought back over everything that had happened since they'd pulled up at Madlen's house. "I guess that's possible." It certainly made more sense than everything being real.

The wolf tilted back its head and howled before attacking. It knocked the sapling from Audrey's hands and she threw herself to the side, trying to grab the sapling before the creature could attack her.

Jordan threw his sapling at the wolf. It went wide.

Audrey grabbed hold of the sapling she'd dropped, spinning to face the wolf. He jumped towards her, a large grey creature with a mouth wide open and filled with sharp teeth. Even though she didn't expect it would help, she raised the sharpened sapling.

Merrick burst into the room and barrelled into the side of the wolf, curved dagger in hand. The air was filled with the scent of baked apples and a metallic smell. Blood streaked his body, none of it seeming to be his. He wrestled with the wolf that snapped and snarled, his dagger sinking into the creature several times. The wolf continued to try and attack, not at all slowed.

Audrey gripped the sapling, wanting to help, but

having no idea what to do. There was no way she could attack the wolf without harming Merrick.

Jordan moved close to Audrey, his attention focused on Merrick and the wolf. "What do we do?"

"I don't know." At a sound behind her, she spun to see another wolf in the doorway. She raised the sapling, pointing the sharp end at the oncoming wolf.

Jordan raised his sapling. Before either of them could do anything, Merrick leapt on the second wolf, more blood streaking his body, several gashes on his chest.

Audrey remained at her brother's side, staring as Merrick fought the wolf, still having no idea how to help. Her hands began to ache from how tightly she gripped the sapling. Several times she thought there was an opening, but before she could attack, the opportunity was lost.

Merrick rose above the wolf, sinking the dagger into it one last time. The creature stilled. Drawing the dagger out, Merrick looked at them.

Chapter Eight

Audrey drew in a sharp breath, taking a step back at the look she saw in Merrick's eyes. A wild, almost feral look. "Merrick?" Her voice was hesitant and she wanted to retreat further. She held her ground, not daring to move in case it startled him.

He remained poised over the wolf, the wild look remaining in his eyes. The sharp scent of blood filled the room.

"Merrick. They're dead."

Merrick stayed where he was a moment longer before leaping past them and disappearing down the stairwell. The scent of baked apples, entwined with a metallic smell, remained behind, slowly dissipating.

Jordan stopped in the doorway. "What happened?"

Audrey slowly shook her head. "I have no idea."

"Think he'll be back?"

"I hope so." She doubted they could survive in this place on their own.

"What are we meant to do with them?" Jordan gestured towards the two dead wolves.

"Why do you think I have all the answers?" she demanded. Her brother took a wary step back from her. She sighed heavily. "Sorry. But I don't know much more than you."

Jordan's gaze remained focused on the wolves. "Do you think we'll be able to return home? That we'll find our parents."

She didn't hesitate to answer. "Yes." She had no idea how, but she'd find a way to return to Madlen's and rescue their parents. "Somehow."

"How did we end up here?"

"Magic."

"That's why you didn't want to tell me anything."

She nodded, eyeing the wolves. She had no idea what to do with them. All they could do was leave the large beasts where they'd fallen, but she didn't want to spend the rest of the night in a room with two dead bodies.

"Are you scared?"

She looked at her brother, seeing the fear and uncertainty on his face. She wished she could tell him no. "We will find a way home." She returned to the fireplace, giving the wolves a wide berth. "I'll keep watch if you want to sleep. We can take turns." She leaned the sapling against the wall so she could add more wood to the fire. There was no way she was going to let it go out. She wanted to see what was coming for them.

Jordan returned to the spot where they'd been sitting earlier, propped against each other asleep. "I don't think I can sleep." He smothered a yawn. "Did those carrots taste like dirt to you before?"

"No." She examined him. "Are you okay?"

He shrugged. "Probably just tired and hungry."

She wanted to check his temperature like their mum did when either of them wasn't well, pressing the palm of her hand against their forehead and then the back of her hand against their cheek. But she didn't move. She wasn't sure she wanted to know if her brother was coming down with something. The problems they already faced seemed overwhelming.

Audrey leaned against the wall, holding the sharpened sapling again. She stared into the flames, struggling to keep her eyes open as the time stretched out. At some stage, Jordan fell asleep and she was tempted to wake him when the fire died down and she had to add more timber. His face was flushed so she left him curled up on the floor and returned to leaning against the wall.

The howl of wolves regularly punctuated the night. She'd no sooner start to nod off, the end of the sapling planted against the floor helping keep her upright, when the wolves would startle her into wakefulness.

Merrick arrived with the dawn, his body coated with blood and the handle of the dagger visible above the top of his boot. He paused in the doorway, the wild look no longer in his eyes. "You are unharmed?"

Her grip on the sapling tightened as she examined his body. "Yeah." She wanted to rush to him and check his wounds. "How bad are you injured?"

"I wanted to see you were unharmed before I cleaned up in the nearby stream." He started to turn away.

"Wait." She took a single step towards him. "You're going to leave us alone again?"

Jordan sat up, rubbing at his eyes. "What's going on?"

"You aren't alone." Merrick glanced at Jordan before returning his attention to Audrey. "I won't be long."

"Where are you going?" Rising to his feet, Jordan stretched.

"He's going to a stream to clean up," Audrey said.

"It isn't far." Merrick remained where he was in the doorway, half turned away from them.

"That sounds nice. Can I come too?" Jordan asked. "I'm boiling hot."

Audrey finally gave in to the urge and pressed her hand against her brother's forehead and then his cheek. "You're sick?"

"It will be from the food he ate at Madlen's," Merrick said.

"You should know better than to eat food you don't know exactly what's in it," Audrey said. "People don't always take allergies seriously. How are we going to get you medical attention around here when all that's out there are trees?"

"It's not from his allergies," Merrick said. "From Fae food. All other food is tasteless or like dust and he will sicken and die if he doesn't continue to eat it."

Audrey examined Merrick, hoping he wasn't serious. But he clearly was. "Is there a cure?"

"It depends on what you consider a cure." He looked from one to the other. "It sounds like you have to watch what you eat anyway. Fae food isn't all that hard to come by in this realm. It's human food that's difficult to find."

"What about when we return to our world? How will we find Fae food?" Audrey asked.

"There's no need for you to return to your world." Merrick glanced towards the stairwell. "I need to wash."

She wanted to protest. "I'll… I'll wait here."

"We should stick together. We've already lost Mum and Dad." Jordan moved closer to her.

"We haven't lost them. We know exactly where they are." She glared at her brother. The word 'lost' made her think of things that were difficult, if not impossible, to find.

"Doesn't matter how you look at it. We still should stick together. The stairwell isn't that narrow," Jordan said.

"It's okay. I'll stay here." She glanced at the doorway, not wanting to look at it too long. All staring at it did was remind her of how lame she was.

"You can't stay up here forever." Jordan gestured towards the doorway. "Eventually, you're going to have to walk down there."

"The timber of the stairs isn't damaged. They're safe to use," Merrick said.

"It's not that," Jordan said. "She's scared of confined spaces. One of our cousins locked her in a wardrobe when she was five."

Merrick crossed the space between him and Jordan unnaturally fast, looming over him. "You will never mention that to anyone again."

Jordan stumbled back from Merrick. "It isn't that big a deal. Only annoying. Like now."

Merrick made a move towards Jordan.

Worried for her brother, she pushed her way between the two of them. She faced Merrick, her hand pressed against his chest, trying not to think of the blood drying on it. "Leave him."

"You would have him put your life in danger because he doesn't know when to remain silent?"

"That doesn't make sense. How can people knowing I'm terrified of confined spaces put my life in danger?" She started to remove her hand from his chest.

He rested a hand over hers, keeping it in place. "Our fears can be used to control us. Contain us. Keep us in place."

"You're telling me, you're afraid of nothing." She didn't bother keeping the disbelief from her voice. Everyone was scared of something.

"Whether or not I'm afraid of anything isn't the point. If I was afraid of something, I wouldn't share the details with anyone."

She shifted back slightly, her hand still resting

under his, surrounded by the warmth of his body. "It doesn't change anything. Regardless of if anyone knows, I am terrified of confined spaces and there's no way you're getting me down that stairwell." She barely had time to register his grin before he was tossing her over his shoulder and dashing down the stairs. It was a faster trip than yesterday. Her feet were touching the ground outside before she had the chance to try and escape.

He grabbed her hands when she struck out at him. "I could not let you remain up there forever." His words were soft and he leaned close to her. "I said I'd never deliberately harm you. Have I harmed you?"

She wanted to say yes. "Let me go." She tugged against his grip, knowing it would be impossible to break free if he chose to hold on.

He let go of her. "You didn't answer the question."

Annoyed with him, she took a step back. "No, I didn't." She held up her hands, smudges of blood on her palms. "Where is the stream?"

He studied her for a moment longer before he stepped back, his expression becoming closed. "This way." He glanced at Jordan, who'd followed them, before leading the way through the trees.

She felt a moment of guilt before she realised why she was so angry with Merrick. She hurried after him.

Stumbling, she came alongside him, trying to keep up with his pace.

He steadied her, slowing down, but remaining silent. He did glance at her, but said nothing.

She had a feeling he'd been about to say something. "Not physically." When he glanced at her in confusion, she continued. "You didn't harm me physically."

He didn't speak immediately, waiting until the stream was in sight and waving Jordan ahead first. He drew her to a stop. "How did I harm you?"

"Would Madlen have harmed you if she'd done nothing to you other than keep you in that room?"

Again he remained silent for a moment. "You felt imprisoned."

Audrey nodded.

"I'm sorry. What would you have preferred I did?" When she didn't speak, he added, "Other than leave you in the cottage."

"I don't know." She sighed heavily. "It's so frustrating. It's been years. You'd think I'd be over it by now."

"What happened?"

Chapter Nine

Audrey met Merrick's gaze, surprised he seemed interested in the answer. "One of my older cousins thought it would be funny to lock me in a wardrobe in the back room of the house we lived in at the time. Everyone was there. I forget what we were celebrating. Another birth, a birthday." She shrugged. "Some family event."

"No one noticed you missing?"

"He told everyone I'd gone next door to play with my friend. She was a year older than me at six." She fell silent. The feeling of being trapped and unable to summon help washed over her. She'd been terrified. "He told me I'd starve to death in there because no one would find me. They wouldn't notice I was gone."

Merrick gathered her hands in his. "Who missed you?"

She smiled fleetingly. "In those days Jordan was never far from me. Always pestering me to play. He saw our cousin put me in the wardrobe. It was an old one and there was a latch at the top he couldn't reach. He brought a stool back with him and clambered up to unhook the latch. When he unlocked the door and swung it open I hugged him so tight he said he couldn't breathe."

"I will protect him for helping you when you needed him." His grip momentarily tightened on her hands. "What happened to your cousin?"

"When my parents learned what had happened, there was a big argument between many of the adults. Some said he was too young to know better, others that it was a harmless prank and some agreed with my parents that it was unacceptable." She smiled again, this one lingering longer. "We never had anything to do with him and his parents again. Jordan and I weren't the only kids who were relieved. He was such a bully. It always amazed me that Jordan helped me instead of running and hiding like he normally did. He was terrified of our cousin. We all were."

"Do you want me to do something about your cousin?" Merrick asked.

She shook her head. "Forget about him." She glanced towards the stream where her brother had removed his sneakers and rolled up his jeans to stand in the shallows.

"It appears you haven't."

"I've forgotten him, just not the experience." She looked down at her hands cradled in his. "I need to wash the blood off." She wondered why she wasn't disgusted or stressed about the blood not only on her, but also on Merrick.

"You're calmer today."

She smiled. "Can you read minds?"

"No. It's merely observation." He let go of one of her hands, continuing to hold her other hand as they walked towards the stream. "The Fae often have human protégés. You don't have to return home."

"How does that work?"

"The Fae is responsible for the care of the human."

"What does the Fae get out of it?"

Reaching the bank of the stream, Merrick turned to face her. "The company of the human when they desire it."

"That doesn't make sense." She frowned, his wording sinking in. "They? When the Fae desires it? What if the human doesn't?"

"There are many different types of human and Fae relationships. I wouldn't ask you to be my protégé if it was to be little more than a pet."

"You keep humans as pets?" She recalled the conversation Madlen had with the nephew. Was this what the human trafficking was about?

"Some do. Not my family. Any humans in our care are there because they wish to be and not because they're little more than slaves."

"No." She drew her hand from his. "I'm not interested in becoming anyone's pet."

"Protégé."

"It doesn't matter what you call it. Not when it's the same thing by the sounds of it." Turning her back on him, she headed for the stream, sitting on the bank to remove her sneakers before wading into the water. She gasped at the cold, hurriedly washing her hands and face before retreating to the bank. "Aren't you cold, Jordan?"

"If I had something else to wear, I'd go for a swim. I'm burning hot and feel like crap." Jordan splashed water onto his face.

Merrick entered the water after removing his boots and leaving the dagger with them on the bank. "There are apple trees further downstream on the opposite bank. Some of them are ripe."

"I can't eat fruit," Jordan said.

"You've never tried Fae fruit." Reaching the middle of the stream, Merrick submerged himself.

Jordan faced Audrey. "Do you think they'd be okay?"

She shrugged. "I don't think you have a choice. Not if you want to live."

"Surely he didn't really mean I'd die. I mean, that's pretty drastic since I only had a handful of toffees."

Merrick rose, water cascading down his body, slicking his hair back from his face. "How much poison does it take to kill someone?"

Jordan paled. "It was poison?"

"For those not Fae it is. And for those without Fae magic." Merrick gestured downstream. "It isn't far and I'll hear you if you call out. But there shouldn't be any trouble at this time of day."

"It was poison?" Jordan stared at Merrick.

Audrey wanted to beg Merrick to say he was joking. But his expression was serious. "Do you want me to go with you, Jordan?"

Jordan slowly shook his head. "Poison." He took several steps in the direction of the apple trees. "No wonder I feel so bad."

Audrey rose to her feet. "Jordan?"

He continued to slowly shake his head. "No. I'm okay. I mean, kind of." He paused a moment. "Poison."

She wanted to hurry after her brother to make sure

he stayed safe. Or as safe as was possible for him to be at the moment. She felt as dazed as Jordan. Her gaze was drawn to Merrick who ran his hands over his chest to remove the last of the blood. Her breath caught in her throat and she was unable to look away. Even when he looked in her direction, his movements stilling.

His gaze roamed her body and he slowly walked towards her, heading for the bank.

She tried to think of something to say. Anything to explain why she stared at him. Other than the obvious one of admiring his body. "Your magic. It didn't-" She stumbled over the words. "It's okay? It didn't do anything to you last night?"

He stopped in front of her, rivulets of water running down his body. "There is something wrong with it. I don't know what, or what it will cause, but there's definitely something wrong."

"How can you tell?"

"My magic has been a part of me my entire life. Do you not know when there's something wrong with your body?"

"I suppose." She was tempted to take a step backwards. He was too close. It seemed better than the other action she was tempted to take. That of running her hands across his chest. She drew in a shuddering breath. "How do you find out what's wrong?"

"Ask those who are better skilled with their magic than I am." He smiled slightly. "Have you forgotten I'm reasonably good at reading body language?" His gaze momentarily dropped to her lips. "You don't have to hide the way you feel from me."

"I will go home eventually."

"It isn't necessary. There's nothing preventing you from remaining here."

She wished she could explain it to him. She couldn't figure out all the words she needed to help him understand exactly what she meant. "I'll never be your protégé."

He lightly ran his fingers across her cheek. "What if I wanted something different?"

"I–" Her mouth went dry while her mind went blank.

His lips curved into a brief smile. "Should I be grateful you didn't instantly say no?"

She was almost relieved to spot Jordan running towards them, two apples held aloft.

As he came closer, Jordan called out, "These are amazing. I've never tasted anything like them before in my life."

Merrick moved close enough she could feel the

heat coming off his body. She looked up, her gaze colliding with his.

"I might not be able to live in your world, but there's nothing stopping me from visiting." He held her gaze a moment longer before striding to his boots.

Jordan came to a halt not far from her. He glanced between the two of them. "What's wrong?"

She shook her head, gesturing towards the apples. "You can eat them? Have you had any of the usual symptoms?"

Jordan shook his head. He held out one of the apples. "You should have one. You can't imagine how amazing it is. Don't you want to be able to eat whatever you want?"

"At what price?"

"None. I feel amazing."

She forced a smile to her lips. She really hoped there were no major repercussions. "That's good."

Jordan's expression fell. "You don't believe that."

"I want to believe it."

"That's not the same."

Merrick joined them. "Time to go. We need to get somewhere more safe, than the cottage before night falls." He held out a carrot to Audrey. "I'm afraid I can't offer more."

"She should have an apple," Jordan said.

Merrick took a menacing step towards Jordan.

Audrey placed a hand on Merrick's arm, relieved when he turned towards her. She slightly shook her head.

Merrick inclined his head, placing his hand over hers for a moment before gesturing in a direction past the cottage. "My family's estate is in that direction. It's too far for us to travel there before nightfall. I know of another place we can reach before then."

Jordan walked on Merrick's right. "What place?"

"A small village a couple of hours from my family's estate. The tavern owner knows my family and will allow us to stay the night," Merrick said.

"A real tavern?" Jordan asked. "That serves alcohol."

"A tavern that serves food your sister can eat." Merrick looked at Audrey. "I'm sorry I have nothing else for you."

She'd finished the carrot quicker than she wished, even with taking extremely small bites. "It happens sometimes. It's nearly impossible to buy food for us when we're out and if something happens to the food we've packed, then we have to go hungry." Which she'd done on quite a few occasions due to various accidents. Although she was still certain the one involving the cousin who'd locked her in the wardrobe hadn't been an accident.

"How far do we have to walk?" Jordan asked.

"We should arrive before nightfall," Merrick said.

"How long before?" Jordan asked.

"Not long." Merrick continued walking, glancing at Jordan as he spoke to him.

Jordan stopped abruptly. "We're walking the entire day?"

Chuckling, Audrey kept walking, looking over her shoulder to see the shocked expression she'd expected on her brother's face. "You might want to ask how many hours there are of daylight. Instead of assuming it's like Brisbane."

Jordan hurried after them. "That's a good idea. How many hours are there?"

"At this time of year, there's approximately twelve hours of daylight."

Jordan groaned. "That sounds worse now I know exactly how many."

She grinned at her brother. "You're welcome." Her smile remained in place at the disgruntled look he gave her.

Chapter Ten

Silence fell amongst them as they plodded towards their destination. They eventually came across a dirt road that was devoid of travellers. Several times they stopped for a break and once Merrick offered to carry Audrey upon his back. Seeing how fatigued he looked, she declined.

By the time they saw the village in the distance, Audrey was ready to collapse and if her brother complained once more she might hit him. Hard enough to bruise. He opened his mouth, closing it when she glared at him.

"Did you want to wait here and I'll go ahead and bring back horses for you?" Merrick asked.

She doubted she'd rise again if she sat down. "It's not far." She'd been chanting that phrase for over an hour. "Tell me they have hot running water and a bathtub I can soak in." From what she could see the place looked like a medieval village with very little in the way of modern facilities.

"Let me carry you," Merrick said.

"You could always carry me," Jordan muttered. "I'm the one who's been sick. And starting to feel terrible again."

She took a step towards her brother, stepping in front of Merrick. "Will you-"

Merrick drew her back, unclenching her fist. "We're nearly there." He kept hold of her hand, slipping his fingers between hers. "What do you want to eat?"

Jordan interrupted Audrey. "Roast."

"Interrupt her again and next time your sister wishes to hit you, I'll hold you for her."

Jordan put space between him and Merrick. "That's her favourite meal. Any roast."

Merrick looked at Audrey. "Is it?"

"That was my brother's way of apologising for being a pain." She gave him a half-hearted glare. "He isn't forgiven though."

Jordan grinned. "Yeah, I am. You're not threatening me with things you'd never do anyway."

"One day," she muttered.

The rest of the walk into the village was silent and Merrick led the way to the tavern, several horses tied up at the water trough out the front, a hitching post by it. Audrey found herself gaping at the sight of the village. Smoke curled into the sky from many of the chimneys, each house seeming to have one. The roads were paved with cobblestone, ruts worn into them from wagon wheels, and there were a scattering of shops at the start of the village with houses beyond them. She tried to count how many buildings, but it was difficult to tell since the village was mostly on flat ground. From what she could tell, there were probably thirty buildings at the most.

Reaching the tavern, Merrick held the door open for Audrey, stepping inside and waiting until Jordan had his hand on the door before he let it go. "I'll organise that bath you desire." He let go of her hand and strode towards the bar.

Audrey slowed to a stop, her brother doing the same. "Not everyone in here is human." She tried not to stare, but it was difficult when she saw what she assumed were Fae as well as creatures that looked human, but had skin with a green tint. There were humans amongst them wearing distinctly medieval clothes.

"Do we have to go home? They get to wear swords here," Jordan said.

"That's probably because they need to use them," Audrey said.

"Oh. I didn't think of that." Jordan's expression fell.

Merrick returned to them, smiling. "I've arranged rooms for each of you and baths." A young woman followed him and he gestured her forward.

The young woman smiled at Jordan. "I'll show you to your room. Are you from the realms of humans?" She looked him up and down. "You wear the type of clothes they often wear."

Audrey smiled as her brother walked beside the young woman, rambling on about where he lived, heading for the stairs on the far side of the room. Her smile faded. "Will he be okay? Fae food won't kill him?"

"As long as he continues to eat it, he'll be fine." Merrick gestured towards the stairs. "Your bath awaits."

"That sounds marvellous." She walked beside him. "How will we get Fae food in our world?"

"I'll see that you have what you need."

She came to a stumbling stop. "My parents. They ate the toffee too."

"I'll see you have enough food for your family."

"Why?"

"It's very little in comparison to saving my life.

They planned to end it when I was no longer of use to them." He cradled her hand in his. "I wouldn't be much of a knight if I denied what you've done for me in an effort to avoid paying back what I owe you."

She wanted to protest that he owed her nothing, but she had no other way of getting the food her family needed.

"You can say it. Whatever it is you wish to say."

She told him the words she'd thought, looking away so she didn't have to see his expression.

He ran his fingers along her cheek with enough pressure to turn her head so she faced him again. "I wouldn't betray your trust." He took a step back, continuing to hold her hand. "I'll show you to your room."

She followed him to the stairs able to go up only one of them before her legs gave way from fatigue.

Merrick scooped her into his arms, the scent of his magic swirling around them.

"Merrick." She pressed her hand against his bare chest as he hurried up the stairs with her. "Set me down. You said you shouldn't use your magic." She breathed in deeply. "The metallic smell seems to be getting stronger." She caught the flicker of wildness in his eyes before it vanished, his arms tightening around her.

He set her down in front of an open door. "I noticed." He kept his arms around her. "The small amount of magic I used then should have made no difference."

She didn't want to move away from him. "What does it mean? The metallic smell."

"I don't know. The barkeep has sent a message to my family. I'm sure they'll have someone who can look into my magic and see what's wrong with it." He glanced past her. "Your bathwater will be cooling."

She reluctantly stepped away from him, not breaking eye contact until she ran into the wall behind her. She glanced away, stepping to the side. He was gone in the few seconds she'd looked away. Peering up and down the hallway didn't help. He was nowhere to be seen. She opened her mouth to call out to him, closing it instead, her gaze resting on each of the closed doors. For all she knew, someone might be asleep.

Stepping into the room, she closed the door, slipping the bolt into place to lock it. Facing the room, she stopped where she was. This was where she was to stay for the night? A large wooden tub was set before a flickering fireplace, a rug between it and the carved timber bed. Several lamps were placed around the room and a small table with two chairs was set at the window in the far corner, a plate of food placed on it. She was half tempted to pinch herself to make sure it was no dream. But the aches and pains she felt from the walk clearly let her know this was real.

Her gaze was drawn between the food and tub. It didn't take her long to make a choice. She was starving, but the aches in her body were worse than the ache in her stomach from lack of food. Shedding her clothes as she hurried towards the tub, she winced as she clambered in, her body protesting the action. The moment she was in the water, some of her aches seemed to fade, the warmth sinking into her body.

She had no idea how he'd managed to organise it all so quickly, but she was extremely grateful. She relaxed in the tub, almost drifting off several times, and possibly nodding off at least once. Slipping in the water once again, she rose to her feet. It was probably safest if she climbed out rather than risk drowning with how exhausted she was. At least now the aches and pains were pretty much gone.

She dried off using the large, thick towel left on the bed and dressed in the medieval clothes set out for her. A simple pair of trousers and a shirt. She took her phone out of her jeans and slipped it into a pocket of her trousers. It was the only item she really needed. The clothes weren't important.

Before she could sit at the table, there was a knock at the door. She opened it to find Merrick, obviously having had a wash. He wore a shirt and trousers that had a medieval look about them and had a sword at his side.

"Are you feeling better after your wash?" Merrick glanced at the tub that sat by the fire.

"Yeah. I can't believe how soaking got rid of all my aches from walking so far."

Merrick smiled. "I asked them to put something in the water for you."

"Are you important around here or something? They seem to have gone to a lot of trouble for you."

"My parents are." He gestured towards the food on the table. "Did you wish to eat up here or down in the tavern?"

"I can eat in the tavern?" She'd expected similar laws to back home and had thought she'd have to eat up here since she wasn't of legal drinking age.

"You can dine wherever you wish."

"The tavern." She turned, planning to collect her food.

Merrick captured her hand, drawing her to him.

"They'll serve you something down there. This was only if you wanted to eat before you washed."

"That seems like a waste."

"They have dogs that will appreciate it." He drew her out of the room. "Your brother is downstairs."

She walked at Merrick's side, clinging to his hand as she checked out the area, stumbling a couple of times since she'd been too busy looking at other things. But there was so much to see, not the least being the many strange people in the tavern.

Jordan rose from his seat, waving them over. He was at one of the larger tables, sitting with a mixture of humans and Fae.

When Audrey started towards the table, Merrick turned her in a different direction, gesturing towards a small table along the side of the room. It was in the shadows where the candlelight from the chandeliers didn't quite reach. She looked between the two tables, nodding at her brother when he smiled and sat back down. Continuing to hold Merrick's hand, she wove her way through the tables and patrons, her gaze drawn to the many strange creatures amongst the humans and Fae. One of them had a bird like look about him.

Reaching the table, Merrick drew out a chair for Audrey, waiting until she was seated before he sat down. They were no sooner seated, then a waitress served them their meal.

"What is it?" Audrey asked.

The waitress remained by the table. "Roast venison and vegetables. No herbs or spices, just plain and simple. And suitable for humans."

"Is that fine?" Merrick asked.

She smiled. "Yes." It took a great deal of effort not to wolf the food down. She was nearly finished eating when a commotion by the front door drew her attention.

Merrick called to the group of male and female Fae, rising from his seat when they started towards him. "I won't be long. They're some of my parents' knights."

Chapter Eleven

Audrey remained at the table, glancing in the direction of her brother a few times. He seemed to be enjoying himself.

Merrick rejoined her at the table, leaving the knights by the front door. "It seems that one of my knights managed to take my niece to safety. Only my sister is missing."

"Do they know where she is?" She placed her cutlery on the empty plate.

Merrick shook his head. "We'll keep looking until we find her." He glanced in the direction of the knights who remained by the front door. "They came to collect us. We can stay at my parents' estate this evening if you wish. Or, if you feel like you've already travelled enough for the day, we can remain here."

She didn't want to go one bit further. "You want

to see your family." Not that she blamed him. If it had been her brother in danger, she would have wanted to check on him too.

"I can wait till morning if you need me to," Merrick said.

"We can go there this evening." The momentary flash of relief she saw in his expression didn't surprise her. "I'll let my brother know." She started to rise.

"No need to disturb him for now. I'll have a carriage arranged for you so you can travel the rest of the distance in comfort." Merrick returned to the knights at the front door.

It took less time than Audrey expected for the carriage to be organised. Merrick handed her inside, joining her and Jordan. It was a quiet trip and when Merrick said they were approaching his family's estate, she peered out the window, mouth dropping open when she realised they were approaching a castle.

She sat back, trying to see Merrick more clearly in the shadowy interior of the carriage. "You live in a castle."

Jordan checked out the window. "That's a castle. We're going to stay in a castle?"

"It's a strong, defensive building," Merrick said.

"A castle."

Merrick laughed softly. "Yes, a castle. It isn't for decoration. We need to defend our estate when others try to take it from us."

The carriage pulled up and Audrey was unable to ask any of the other questions she had. Her and Jordan were hurried away as Merrick's family descended upon him.

The trip through the castle was a blur and Audrey was shown to a room next to the one her brother was shown to. After being told that if she needed anything to ask, she was left alone. The room was spacious and silent, yet it felt too small and confining. Discovering a door leading onto a balcony, she stepped outside. She was still standing out there when Merrick joined her.

He remained in the doorway, gesturing behind him. "I knocked and was concerned when you didn't answer."

She faced him, leaning against the railing of the balcony, the stone cool against her back. "Your niece is okay?"

He nodded. "I'm sorry I wasn't able to show you to your room and left it to others to do so."

She wanted to ask him what was wrong. Wanted to know why he sounded so formal. "It's okay. Your family wanted to see that you were unharmed." Her gaze was drawn to his chest covered by his shirt. "Or at least not seriously injured."

"If I'd used my magic, I could have easily repaired the damage the wolves did to my body."

"What is wrong with your magic?" Audrey asked.

"I'm showing signs of iron sickness. Probably from the length of time I was in Madlen's home."

"What's iron sickness?" She wished now she'd remained inside where there was more light so she could see him more clearly.

"We Fae can't handle iron based metals or be around them for long periods of time. It causes a sickness and eventually we die."

"You're dying?" She automatically took a step forward and started to reach for him. She lowered her hand.

He closed the distance between them, capturing her hand. "No. If I stay away from iron, I'll recover."

"What is your sword made of?"

He chuckled. "You don't need to worry. My sword is made from one of the Fae metals. No iron in it at all." His grip momentarily tightened on hers. "I'm flattered by your concern."

"Where was the iron in Madlen's house?" She tried to picture everything she'd seen.

"Buildings in your realm are full of it. Even the nails you use contain iron."

"Oh." She'd planned to ask him to take them back to Madlen's house. Her and Jordan needed to find their parents.

"Is something wrong?" He paused a moment. "Or were you concerned you'd never be able to see me again." He pressed a finger against her lips when she started to speak. "If you're about to say no, I'd rather you left me wondering than to dash my hopes so soon."

Her lips curved into a smile beneath the light pressure of his finger. She turned her head enough to dislodge it. "I wasn't about to say anything about you visiting me." Her smile faded. "I need to return to Madlen's house. My parents are there. Do you think you can find someone to take me?"

"Unless they've been there previously, or you can picture it clearly, it will be impossible for anyone else to take you there."

"We won't be able to go back to Madlen's?" There had to be a way to find her parents. Besides wanting them in her life, she had no idea how she could explain to anyone what had happened.

"I'll take you there. Your brother can remain

behind and I can take one of my knights with me to help rescue your parents."

For a few seconds, she thought she hadn't heard correctly. Or that she might have heard what she wanted to hear. "We can rescue my parents?"

"Yes."

Drawing her hand from his, she threw her arms around him. "Thank you. Thank you so much." She realised almost immediately what she'd done and let go of him, taking a step back. "I'm sorry. That was-"

Merrick interrupted her. "That was a thank you that you can repeat any time you wish."

A wry smile formed. "You're very nice." She'd been caught up in the moment and had treated him like one of her close friends.

"Did you forget I can't lie?"

She opened her mouth several times, but nothing came out.

Merrick closed the distance between them again, sliding his arms around her waist to draw her against him. "Did you want me to show you where I was hoping that thank you would lead?"

She didn't need him to explain what he meant this time. She continued to stare up at him, trying to decide her course of action. When he started to draw away from her, she slid her hands over his chest and linked them behind his neck, keeping him close to her. "I don't belong in your world."

"How would you know? You've seen very little of the realms of the Fae."

"I have a life back in my world. A world you said you can't live in." She knew she should let him go, but what she really wanted to do was so far from that, it might as well be the opposite. She wanted to kiss him. Just once. Were Fae different to humans?

"You could have a life in this realm." His arms momentarily tightened around her. "It wouldn't have to include me. My family would make you welcome for as long as you wished to stay. They're extremely grateful you helped me escape."

"We helped each other escape."

"I'd like to think I could have managed to get out of there somehow, but I know it would have been impossible for me to escape without help."

Coming to a decision, she rose onto the tip of her toes. "I'm not staying."

He tilted his head towards her. "That might change in the future."

The door of the bedroom burst open. "Aude. What are-" Jordan was halfway across the room before he spotted her, breaking off as he did.

She pulled out of Merrick's arms, initially feeling

guilty. That was quickly followed by annoyance and she glared at her brother. "Haven't you heard of knocking?"

"I did. You mustn't have heard." Jordan remained in the doorway leading onto the balcony. "Don't you care that woman still has Mum and Dad?"

"Of course I do."

"The issue has been discussed. We'll collect them tomorrow," Merrick said. "Audrey and I."

"You will?" Jordan asked. "How?"

"The same way we left there. With magic." The scent of Merrick's magic filled the area, the metallic smell still present. He held out an autumn leaf to Audrey that had formed on his palm. The edges were curled and blackened. "If you need me, whisper my name against it then let it go." He placed it in her hand when she didn't take it. "Or, if all you wish to do is talk to me, whisper against it while avoiding saying my name. I'll hear what you have to say."

"Cool. Can I see it?" Jordan gestured towards the leaf Audrey held.

"No," Merrick said flatly.

"Should you be doing magic?" Audrey closed her hand over the leaf, surprised it didn't crumble at her action. "What about your iron sickness?"

"The less magic I have, the less the iron sickness

will affect me. Which is probably why I've only been slightly affected and didn't realise I had it."

"So it's okay if you use your magic?" Audrey slipped the leaf into a pocket.

"Yes."

"Can I go with the two of you?" Jordan asked. "I want to help."

"No," Merrick stated.

"They're my parents too," Jordan said.

"The less people, the less likely we are to be caught," Merrick said.

"Should I stay behind too?" She forced herself to speak, even though she didn't want to make the offer. She could completely understand Jordan's comment. They were her parents.

"You'll need to show me which of the humans are your parents." He took a step away from her. "We'll leave once we've had a sleep and something to eat in the morning."

"Will that be too long? Should we go after them now?" Audrey asked.

"We need time to rest. As does my knight. We want the best chance of success."

"Okay." Once again it was an effort to speak the word and she would have preferred to argue. She didn't want her parents to spend too much time with Madlen.

"It isn't okay," Jordan said. "We should be going after them right now."

Merrick faced Jordan. "So we can all be captured? How would that help rescue your parents?"

"What if you're too late?" Jordan demanded.

"Waiting is the best chance." Merrick turned to Audrey. "I'll see you in the morning."

Chapter Twelve

Audrey watched Merrick leave, not sure if she should be relieved or annoyed that Jordan had interrupted them.

Jordan moved close to her, keeping his voice low. "What did you think you were doing? He's not human."

"You seemed to be getting pretty friendly with some of the Fae at the tavern."

"Yeah, that was until I saw how most of them treated the humans with them. They treat them like slaves. One of them wanted to know who my master was so he could see if he was willing to sell me. We don't belong here, Aude."

"They're not all the same." She refused to believe Merrick would treat a human like that. Look how he'd been with her. Although he had asked her to be his protégé. That certainly wouldn't suit her.

"Do you think Mum and Dad will be okay?" Jordan asked.

She stared at her brother as she tried to figure out what to say. He looked so young and uncertain. Like he was years younger than her, not just eighteen months. "We haven't been gone long."

"I suppose."

She glanced past him to the bed. "I should probably have a sleep. Who knows what will happen tomorrow."

"Maybe you shouldn't go. They wouldn't want you to risk yourself," Jordan said.

"That's too bad. I'm not about to wait around for something to happen to them. Even you would go if you could."

"What if something happens to you too? What if you don't return? What if I'm the only one left?"

She tried to smile reassuringly, but doubted she'd managed more than a grimace. "I guess you come after me."

Jordan nodded. "I will." He stood there a moment longer before he strode from the room, closing the door behind him.

Audrey didn't make her way to the bed straight away. She stood there far too long, worried about what would happen tomorrow. Not that kicking off her sneakers and climbing into bed helped much. It took her ages to fall asleep. All the things that had happened tumbled through her mind, mixed with the many things that might go wrong.

She was dragged from sleep the next morning by a knock on the door. It took her a few seconds to realise where she was. Everything came crashing in on her. "Yes?" She stumbled out of bed, making her way to the door.

"Would you like me to escort you to the dining room?"

She opened the door to find Merrick looking ready for battle with a sword at one side, a quiver at the other and a bow at his back. "Should I have weapons too?"

"Can you use any?"

She shook her head.

"Then until you learn, it's probably best you don't." He gestured along the hallway. "Are you hungry?"

"Yeah." She slipped back into the room and put her sneakers on, wishing she had another change of clothes. The ones she wore were rumpled from being slept in all night.

Merrick led the way to the dining room where Jordan was already seated. Once they'd traded good mornings, the meal was silent, a knight joining them towards the end. Merrick introduced him as Luw. But even his arrival didn't cause conversations to begin.

Finished her breakfast, she placed her cutlery on her plate, trying not to think about what was to come. If she did, she might not be able to bring herself to return to Madlen's house.

Merrick rose from the table. He held out a hand to Audrey. "Are you ready?"

'No' didn't seem to be the right word, even though it was the one she most wanted to say. "Yeah." She rose, placing her hand in his.

Merrick formed an autumn leaf in his other hand, holding out his arm so Luw could hold onto his forearm. He crushed the leaf in his hand. The world shimmered, reforming to become the bedroom Jordan had used at Madlen's house.

Letting go of Merrick's hand, Audrey hurried across the room to peer out the open doorway, ignoring Merrick's whispered orders not to rush off. She had no plans to run head first into danger. She looked in both directions of the hallway. It was clear. She hurried to the room her parents had stayed in. The bed was made and it looked like no one had ever stayed there. She remained frozen in the doorway, trying to take it all in. What were they meant to do now? How would she find them?

Merrick stopped beside her. "We'll search the house."

Luw placed his hand on Merrick's shoulder. "You should return to the castle. It's too dangerous for you to be wandering around and we have no idea what to expect."

Merrick grinned. "Just because you believe something, doesn't make it true." He turned to Audrey. "Are you coming with me or waiting here?"

There was no way she was about to be left behind. "Madlen was talking about using my parents to experiment on. What does that mean?"

"They were trying to find a cure for iron sickness. I heard them talk about humans being kept in the basement." He headed towards the stairs, glancing over his shoulder.

Audrey hurried after him. They were keeping people locked in a basement? If he'd told her that sooner, she would have demanded he bring her back last night.

Luw followed behind them, sword held ready. "This isn't right. We should return for more knights and warriors."

"We don't know how much time that might cause

to pass." Merrick checked around a corner before he continued.

"Does it take longer to travel by magic that it feels like it does?" Audrey asked.

Merrick stopped at a door at the back of a kitchen. "No. Time doesn't pass equally between the two realms."

She frowned, trying to figure out what he meant. "How is it different?"

"Time tends to pass faster in the human realm than in the realms of the Fae. Very rarely is it slower." Merrick tried to open the door. "It's locked."

Luw stepped forward. "Let me." He took out a white crystal and held it against the door.

Audrey heard a click a moment before Luw opened the door. "How did you do that?"

"The crystal has been imbued with a spell to unlock basic locks." Luw momentarily held it up before he tucked it away in his belt pouch and started down the stairs.

Audrey followed the two knights, closing the door behind her and trying to see past their broad shoulders to what was below. It was impossible. The only thing she could see were the timber stairs she walked down, the brick walls of the basement on her left and a dim light bulb hanging from the ceiling and casting a soft glow.

Reaching the bottom of the stairs, relieved they hadn't been enclosed like the ones at the cottage, Audrey stepped around Merrick. She came to a complete halt. On the far wall of the basement were six cages, each containing a human in various conditions. The only items in each cage were a blanket and a bucket in the corner. Audrey shuddered. It was a good thing her brother hadn't come with them. He would have been even less impressed with the Fae.

One of the humans, curled up in a blanket and lying on the floor, sat up. "Audrey?" Joan struggled to untangle herself from her blanket. "She wouldn't let me see any of you. Not Jordan, not you and not your father. Are you okay? What about your brother? Have you seen him or your father?"

Audrey remained frozen to the spot, unable to speak. Her mum looked dreadful. If this was how she looked after two days, it was a good thing she'd found her before any more time passed.

"Audrey? Are you okay? You can't imagine how worried I've been locked up down here for the past five days. Or at least I think it's been five days."

She took an unsteady step towards her mum. "Five

days?" The words were soft enough they wouldn't have travelled to the cages.

Merrick placed a hand on her shoulder, holding her lightly. "We'll get your mother out of here and find your father."

Joan, who'd been holding onto the bars, backed away. "I can't leave. She said she'd hurt each of you if I tried to leave." She slowly shook her head. "I have to stay here."

"No." Audrey drew out of Merrick's grip, rushing forward to clutch the bars of the cage. "I'm not leaving you here. Jordan is safe and so am I. He'd never forgive me if I left you behind."

Joan took half a step forward. "Jordan is safe too?"

Audrey nodded. "I'll take you to him.

Joan backed away again, pressing her back against the other side of the cage. "The two of you are to go home. Call Patty and tell her you don't know what happened to us. I won't have anyone else caught in this predicament. You can stay with her, Aunt Joan and your great-grandmother."

"No." Audrey wasn't about to leave her mum in a cage.

Merrick moved to her side. "Do you know where she's keeping your husband?"

Joan shook her head, gesturing to the other cages.

The occupants had either not moved or barely glanced at them. "They've been in here a lot longer than me and each has someone they care about held captive somewhere else." Joan came away from the far side of the cage. "How did you escape? You and Jordan."

Anger mixed with the fear and worry Audrey felt. "I didn't eat any of the toffee." Her grip tightened on the bars. "Why did you have to eat the toffee?"

"Your father tried one and he said they tasted amazing. I'd only planned to have one." Her voice trailed off. "I woke up in here."

"Mum-"

Joan interrupted her. "I want you safe. You and Jordan." She came forward to wrap a hand around Audrey's where it gripped the bar. "As long as you two are safe, that's all that matters."

"You're going to desert us? You're going to remain in here while we're out there trying to figure things out on our own?" Audrey demanded.

"Do you expect me to let your father die so I can escape?" Joan asked.

"No, but…" Audrey's voice trailed off. She had no idea what to say. She didn't want either of her parents killed. "There has to be something we can do."

Merrick drew her back from the cage. "Audrey, we have to leave."

She pulled away from him and the cage. "I'm not about to desert my mum." She glared at him.

Merrick slowly approached her. "We can come back later. We'll try and figure out where Madlen is keeping your father and rescue the two of them." He held out his hand.

Chapter Thirteen

She took several steps, backing away towards the stairs. "What about them?" She vaguely gestured towards the rest of the cages. "Are we going to leave them too?"

Luw strode past the front of the cages. "Does anyone want to leave? I can take two with me."

One woman struggled to sit up. "Me. Many more days and I'm dead anyway. If I die, so does he. Madlen has told me that so many times." Her words were broken, her breathing laboured.

Luw took the crystal out of his belt pouch and used it on the cage door. Once he'd returned it to his belt pouch, he opened the door and gathered the woman up off the floor. Carrying her, he continued past the front of the cages. "Anyone else?" Two ignored him and one shook her head. He turned to Merrick. "I'll meet you at the castle." The scent of his magic filled the air and he vanished, taking the woman with him.

"You're not to go with them," Joan ordered. "You need to go home."

"Then I guess you're going to have to come with me if you want to make sure I go home," Audrey said.

"Don't do this," Joan pleaded. "Do not do this."

Audrey wanted to beg the same. Before she could speak, Merrick wrapped his arms around her, dragging her under the stairs with him, pressing her against the wall in the shadows. He clamped a hand over her mouth when she opened hers, about to demand he let her go.

"Someone is opening the door."

His breath brushed across her cheek and she stilled against him, closing her eyes as she tried not to think about the confined space he'd dragged her into. It didn't help. She wanted to fight and struggle and race out of the cramped space under the stairs. Her heart raced and her breath came quick. She couldn't stay here.

Merrick's arms tightened around her. "Don't move."

His whisper was so quiet she barely heard it. The words didn't help. She wanted to run. Fight. Didn't he understand she couldn't stay here?

Footsteps sounded above them on the stairs. They stopped halfway down. "This can't be good."

Audrey recognised the voice of the nephew and she completely agreed with him. This wasn't good. She needed to get out of here. She tried to struggle against Merrick's grip on her. He held her too tightly, his hand remaining clamped over her mouth so she couldn't make a sound. A scream echoed in her mind, but she had no way of releasing it.

The nephew continued the rest of the way down the stairs. "You. You standing there. What happened?"

"Someone came and took her away," Joan said. "She tried to stop them. She was too weak. She was worried about her partner. They didn't listen."

"Who were they?" the nephew demanded.

Audrey alternated between wanting to tell her mum to tell him the truth in case her lies were discovered and wanting to escape. She couldn't do either.

"Not human. They had those pointy ears," Joan said.

"Madlen is going to want to hear about this." The nephew hurried up the stairs, his feet loud against the timber. "This is going to be very bad."

The moment Merrick's grip on her relaxed,

Audrey shot out from under the stairs, turning to glare at him. "Don't you ever–"

He was in front of her in a flash, his hand clapping over her mouth again. "He hasn't gone far."

She turned her head away from him, his hand shifting off her mouth. "You can take my mum. They'll think it's the same person. Dad will be safe. He'll be safe from them thinking Mum deliberately left him behind." She turned towards Joan who was shaking her head. "You can't stay here."

Merrick formed an autumn leaf, the scent of his magic a mixture of baked apples and a metallic undertone that was increasing in strength. He stood where he was for a moment, eyes closed, jaw tightening.

He looked like he fought against something and Audrey was about to ask him what was wrong when he opened his eyes and spoke.

"We're leaving. I said I'd protect you and remaining here is going to get you caught." He reached for her.

She caught a glimpse of a wild look in his eyes, gone almost as soon as she noticed it. A sound from upstairs caught her attention and the scent of his magic caused a rush of fear to wash over her. "Are you crazy?" Her words were a low hiss as she waved her hands through the air. "They'll smell your magic. Are you trying to get my mum killed?"

Merrick captured one of her hands. "That won't help. The smell will fade when it's ready."

She drew away from him. "It better fade before Madlen comes down here." She kept her voice low, as Merrick was also doing.

"Take her out of here," Joan said softly. "You seem to care what happens to her. So take her out of here."

The sound of approaching footsteps had Merrick dragging Audrey back under the stairs, his arms tightening around her when she struggled. "Don't fight me and I won't use my magic to take us out of here."

She tried to hold herself completely still. It was impossible. She wanted to escape. Couldn't remain beneath the stairs a moment longer. The walls pressed in on her and she tried to find something to focus on other than how cramped the area was.

"What did they want?" Madlen reached the bottom of the stairs. "Tell me."

"Your secrets," Joan said.

Madlen laughed. "If they think they'll gain them by stealing one of my experiments, then they have no idea what I'm doing here. No one can gain my secrets so easily."

"How can you be sure of that?" Joan asked.

Madlen came close to the cage, running her fingers across the bars. "Think I would fall for any of your tricks? My secrets are of no use to a human. Only the Fae. And they will give me whatever I want when I finally work everything out. I'm getting so close. So very close." She turned away.

"Unless you keep all your notes in your head, then someone can get to them," Joan said.

Madlen looked over her shoulder. "They're always on me so they might as well be in my head." Laughing, she headed up the stairs. "Nephew. Feed the experiments and find me a replacement human. Another pair. There's no point bringing me only one like you did the previous time. I need a control subject to compare the one I experiment on against." She paused at the top of the stairs. "I have to track down another Fae no one wants." She laughed again. "Or is willing to sell like the last one." She entered the kitchen, her steps brisk.

Audrey, who'd continued to struggle against Merrick, stilled when his arms tightened around her.

He loosened his grip almost immediately, waiting until the door was closed before he spoke. "We're leaving."

Before she could protest, the world shimmered and

reformed around them, She drew away from him, glancing around to find they were in the dining room of the castle. "Take me back." She faced Merrick, taking a step away from him at the look she saw in his eyes. A wild look that made him seem like he was a completely different person.

He closed his eyes, his hands tightening into fists as he lowered his head.

"Merrick?"

He didn't answer immediately, shaking his head slowly as he opened his eyes and took several steps away from her.

"What is wrong?" Her anger at him faded, replaced by worry.

"I will be fine."

"Don't give me that rubbish. You're not fine. I saw you."

"It's the iron sickness. I probably shouldn't have gone back to your world so soon."

Her heart sank. She needed to return to her world. How else was she to find her dad and rescue her mum?

Merrick closed the distance between them, raising a hand as if to touch her. He lowered his hand. "I'm sorry we had to leave your mother behind. I'll have my knights see what they can learn about Madlen and what she's up to. And to find out if there's any connection between her and the attack on me and my sister."

The last of her anger faded. She'd forgotten he had someone missing too. "Do you mean Luw?"

"Two of them escaped. I also need to find out what happened to the rest of my people. My parents have offered me the services of several of their knights." This time, when he reached for her, he captured her hand and cradled it in his. "We will find the ones we seek."

"How do you know?"

"Because we won't stop looking until we find them."

Jordan strode into the room, looking at each of them. "Did you find them? Did you find Mum and Dad?"

She couldn't bring herself to say the words and destroy the hopeful look in his eyes. "I spoke to Mum."

"Is she okay?"

"She told us to go home and forget about them. To ring Aunt Patty."

Jordan's eyes narrowed. "You better not be thinking about doing that."

"Of course not." Surely he knew her better than that.

"Then what are we doing?"

"Getting them away from Madlen." She had no idea how, but they'd figure it out eventually. She turned to Merrick. "How long will it take for your knights to find out some information?"

Merrick shrugged. "It's impossible to say."

A Fae ran into the dining room. "My lord. Your parents are following up on a lead and one of your knights has returned. She's in a bad way and says she knows where your sister is."

"Where is my knight?" Merrick demanded.

"In the foyer. She collapsed, but refuses to be moved until she speaks to you."

"Find Luw." Merrick strode from the room.

Audrey hurried after him. "Will our dad be wherever your sister is?"

Jordan kept pace with Audrey. "I want to come with you this time."

"As far as I know, the two matters have nothing to do with each other." Merrick didn't slow his pace.

Audrey struggled to keep up with him. "Once your sister is safe, does that mean you'll be able to spend more time helping us look for our dad?"

"It won't change anything. Even if we don't find

my sister, people will continue to try and find your father," Merrick said.

"Will he be in our world or your world?" Audrey asked.

"Are there any other worlds?" Jordan came alongside Merrick.

"None that matter." Merrick stepped into the foyer and stopped in front of a Fae. He crouched at her side, waving back the two Fae attending her. "I was worried you'd died, Betsan. Luw and Sayer survived. Do you know if anyone else did?"

Chapter Fourteen

Audrey stared at the Fae who was covered in blood, had torn clothes and damaged armour and poorly mended wounds. Her black hair was plaited back from her narrow face, numerous strands having come loose to fall around her face and shoulders. "She needs a doctor."

Betsan struggled to rise. "It was a slaughter. They knew we were coming and exactly how many we'd be."

Merrick rested a hand on her shoulder. "Don't get up. Do you know who it was?"

Betsan looked up at him, not answering immediately. "It was Tanwen's brother-in-law."

"Are you sure?" When Betsan nodded, Merrick said, "It was Gower."

Again Betsan nodded.

"She needs medical help." Audrey took several steps forward. "Merrick. You have to call a doctor for her."

Merrick rose to his feet, beckoning the Fae forward. "See that someone skilled in healing attends her."

Betsan tried to rise. "Merrick. Wait. Your niece-"

Merrick interrupted her. "Siani is safe. Luw managed to bring her to my parents. You can relax now. Your job is done."

Betsan smiled wryly. "When do I ever relax?"

Merrick chuckled. "Try and make an exception this time."

Betsan laughed, the sound cut off by a sharp, indrawn breath.

The Fae who'd been attending her when they entered the foyer gathered her up and took her, protesting, from the room.

"Will she be okay?" Audrey stared in the direction Betsan had been taken, even though she could no longer see her.

Merrick inclined his head. "I'll make certain of it."

When he formed an autumn leaf, Audrey grabbed hold of his arm. "Where are you going?"

"To visit Gower."

She tightened her grip on his arm when he tried to pull away. "Are you crazy?" Seeing the look in his eyes, she thought it was quite possible he was. "What do you expect to do? Ask him if he has your sister? Why would he tell you? Or let you have her if he does?"

Merrick momentarily closed his eyes, slowly shaking his head. When he opened them, the wild look was gone. "I need Luw here, but I don't have time to wait for him to return."

"There has to be something we can do." Audrey continued to hold his arm, worried he'd leave.

He met her gaze. "We?"

She smiled, a brief one that faded before it had barely formed. "You saved us as much as I saved you."

"No. You could have walked out of that house and never looked back. I was tied and weakened. It was impossible for me to leave."

"As if I'd leave my family behind." She frowned when the wild look returned to his eyes. "Are you okay?"

"It's the iron sickness." He took a step away from her, glancing at her hand on his arm. "I need to go."

"Not without me." She needed to find out more about iron sickness. Needed to know if that was all that was wrong with him.

"And me," Jordan said.

Merrick slowly shook his head. "I can't take two. I need to be able to bring my sister back."

"Jordan can stay here, but I'm going with you." She didn't bother telling him it was because she was worried he wouldn't make it back. He obviously wasn't thinking clearly.

"You want to come with me."

"Yes." She ignored her brother's protests, smiling up at Merrick. "Can you take us to somewhere near where Gower lives?"

"He has a mansion on the outskirts of the town closest to Siani's castle."

"She has a castle?" Audrey heard her brother echo her words, using the same tone of surprise and disbelief she used. "A castle."

"She inherited it from her father when he died a few months ago," Merrick said.

"A castle." Audrey struggled to get her head around the idea.

"Who gets it if she dies?" Jordan asked.

"Gower," Merrick stated.

"He would kill his own niece?" Audrey demanded.

The wild look was back in Merrick's eyes. "Why don't we find out?"

Before Audrey could protest, the world shimmered around them and reformed. They were on the outskirts of a town, standing in the middle of a cobblestone road in front of a mansion. "Are you crazy." She dragged Merrick with her to the side of the road, pulling them close to a tree with widespread branches. The scent of his magic hung in the air. She frowned. "Is that metallic smell getting worse?" She met his gaze, drawing in a sharp breath at the look in his eyes. "Merrick." The wild look had grown worse.

He shook his head, raising a hand to rub his temple. "I need to find Tanwen."

"Merrick?" She clung to his arm when he would have pulled away. "What is wrong?"

He shook his head again, the wild look fading from his eyes, leaving him appearing dazed. "It must be the iron sickness."

"Are you sure? How long does it take to go?"

Merrick shrugged. "I've never had it before."

"Should you wait until it's out of your system before you use your magic?" She had no idea what to do. This world with its magic and strange people was a mystery to her. One she was starting to think she might have enjoyed exploring if her parents weren't in danger.

"If I continue to use my magic it'll weaken the iron sickness."

She studied his face. "Then maybe it's not iron

sickness. Whatever it is, it seems to get worse each time you use your magic."

"It can't be anything else." He tried to pull away from her.

She tightened her grip on him, refusing to let him walk into danger. "What other sicknesses do the Fae get?"

"We aren't like humans. Our magic keeps us healthy. But it's also what makes us sicken when we're around iron too long." He looked pointedly at her hand on his arm, meeting her gaze again before he spoke. "Let me go, Audrey. I have to find my sister."

"You can't walk in there and confront him on your own. That's crazy."

"Would you leave your brother a prisoner?"

"I wouldn't get myself caught trying to rescue him. Then how would I get him to safety." She tried not to think about how she'd behaved when they were in Madlen's basement.

He gave her a look that clearly told her he was remembering the basement. "If you had magic, there is no way you would have been able to speak that sentence."

A smile escaped, fading as quickly as it had come. "Maybe not, but I wasn't thinking clearly. Nor are you right now. We need to find out if he has her, but not by marching in there and demanding to know."

"What do you suggest?"

She struggled to think of an answer. "What are the options?"

"See, even you don't know what to do."

"I didn't say that. I just thought you'd have an idea about other options that you might want me to consider." She barely managed not to protest the look of disbelief he gave her.

"If I can't go in there and demand where my sister is, then I don't know what other options I have."

"That isn't an-" She broke off. "Oh."

"What?"

A smile slowly formed. "We can go in there. Not to demand where your sister is. But to let them know your niece is okay. Siani is his niece too. Wouldn't it be right to let him know?"

"How will that help?"

"You could send me out of the room to wait for you while you let him know Siani is okay, but that your sister isn't." When he stared at her, she had the urge to take a step back and demand what he was thinking. She remained where she was. "I can wander around and see what I can discover. It wouldn't be the first time I've gone off looking for a bathroom only to become lost."

"How will you know what you're looking for?"

She started to shrug, deciding that letting him know she had no idea what to look for might have him returning to his earlier plan. "How does Gower treat humans?"

"Like they're worthless and only there to serve him."

She almost backed out of the plan. But she needed Merrick's help to find her parents. And he obviously needed someone to keep him from doing something stupid. "Thank you for not letting me be caught earlier."

Once more he stared at her for a moment before speaking. "That is why you're helping me?"

She grinned fleetingly. "Only one of the many reasons." She glanced towards the mansion. "Are you ready?"

Merrick inclined his head, tugging his arm from her grip. "Follow me. Don't speak to me and don't meet anyone's gaze. If anyone asks who you belong to, tell them you're my protégé."

"Okay." She didn't like that part of the plan.

"Are you sure you want to go ahead with this?"

She nodded. "Lead the way." She met his gaze,

worried when she saw the look of wildness deep in his eyes. Had he always had that look, or was it something to do with the iron sickness? Or whatever the problem was.

He held her gaze a moment longer before he inclined his head and stepped away from the tree, striding towards the mansion.

She hurried after him, following in his wake. She walked behind and slightly to the side so she could see the building they approached. Drawing near, she noticed numerous warriors patrolling the grounds. Or maybe they were knights. She wasn't certain. Was there a way to tell the difference? If there was, she didn't know what it was.

The front door opened as Merrick approached and a human bowed, gesturing him inside. "My lord Gower has been informed of your arrival, Lord Merrick."

Merrick didn't reply, only followed the man who led the way to the drawing room. He barely glanced at the man when he bowed then hurried away.

Chapter Fifteen

Audrey stopped just inside the doorway, struggling to mask her expression. She wasn't sure which caught her attention more. The drawing room with its antique looking furniture and exquisite wall hangings or the Fae who stood by the fireplace.

Gower's hair was so fair it was white and his frame was tall and narrow, his features angular, his green eyes extremely pale in colour. He wore a sword at his side, but his clothes made him look like he was ready to go to a dinner party. Particularly his embroidered waistcoat. He didn't even glance in Audrey's direction.

Merrick stopped not far from Gower. "Might I have a word with you? It involves our niece."

Gower made a vague gesture that could have been anything from 'go ahead' to 'if you must'.

Merrick half turned so he could see Audrey. "You

may wait outside the room. Close the door on your way out."

It took a few seconds for the words to register. Nodding, she did as he said and closed the door once she was out of the room. A glance in both directions showed no one was in sight. She had no idea where to go. What had she been thinking? Obviously not much at all. How was she meant to discover anything? She didn't know the layout of the place, the routine, what the residents were like or where they'd keep a prisoner.

Having no idea where to start, she randomly headed towards the right. The couple of people she encountered during her wanderings barely glanced at her. She kept her head down and her gaze on the floor each time. The first time it had happened, she barely managed to suppress a grin. Didn't they care? Was it normal for humans to wander around this place?

Coming upon a set of stairs, she headed up them. At the top of the stairs, she arrived at a hallway that led in one direction. Having no other idea what to do, she started along it, glancing in rooms as she passed them. Luckily, all the doors were open and she didn't have to worry about explaining herself if she opened one to find someone on the other side.

The place seemed empty. Like downstairs, it was filled with antique furniture and expensive looking ornaments, statues and wall hangings. She had no idea how much time had passed and wished she could check her phone. Or that she owned a watch.

She found another set of stairs. Narrow ones leading upwards, between two walls. About to turn away from them, knowing she wouldn't be able to manage heading up them, she heard voices. A glance around showed the stairs were the only option if she didn't want to be seen. But surely that shouldn't matter. No one had cared when they'd spotted her downstairs. The voices came closer and she was finally able to make out what they said.

"Half her luck if she's managed to run away. Should we really be looking this hard for her?" a female voice asked.

They were looking for her? She staggered forward, trying to force herself up the stairs. She couldn't do it. Her legs gave way and she huddled at the base of them.

"You search under the bed while I check behind the drapes," a second female voice said. It was sharper than the first voice. "We'll be the ones thinking about fleeing if we don't do as ordered."

"I always think about it. If I had somewhere to run to, I would," the first voice said.

"Hush," the second voice said. "Don't go letting others hear you say that."

"It's not like it'll make any difference," the first voice said, a bitterness to her tone.

"This room is empty. We'll check the next one."

Footsteps sounded closer and Audrey struggled to force herself up the stairs, unable to rise to her feet. She squeezed her eyes tightly closed rather than focus on the walls pressing in on her. Somehow, it helped. She focused on the timber stairs beneath her hands, the wood smooth. She thought of the previous stairs, the sweeping expanse that led upwards. They'd been easy to use since they'd had no walls closing in on them.

Her movements slowed as she thought of the walls surrounding her. A shudder ran through her and this time she focused on how smooth the timber was. Step by step she made her way upwards, barely registering the conversation between the two women, only noting that their voices drew closer.

She reached for the next step, finding emptiness instead. Forcing herself to open her eyes, she found herself kneeling on the floor of a narrow hallway. Her breath caught in her throat and she struggled to remain where she was. Not that she knew where she could go. Behind was the narrow stairwell, in front an equally narrow hallway. Staggering to her feet, she stumbled towards a closed door. Her hand closed over the doorknob and she tried to open it. Nothing. It didn't budge. Her breath came quicker and her grip tightened on the doorknob. She rattled at the door, trying to pull it open, hoping that the room would be more spacious than the hallway.

"Please? Is someone out there? Please. I need to know where I am."

Audrey froze, her heart still racing and her breath coming too fast. She turned slightly, still pressed against the door, looking towards the direction the voice had come from.

"Are you still there?" The voice caught on the words.

Audrey staggered the short distance towards the next door, trying the doorknob and finding it locked as well. "I'm here." She leaned against the timber. Closing her eyes, she tried to slow her breathing.

"Please. Can you take a message to my family? I need to get out of here and find out if my daughter and brother survived."

A mixture of fear and excitement rushed through

her. Surely she hadn't found Merrick's sister. "Who are you?"

There was a lengthy silence before the woman answered. "Tanwen."

Audrey drew in a deep breath, struggling to remain calm. Or at least maintain some kind of calm. "They're safe."

Again there was silence before the woman spoke. "How can I trust you? How do you know my family?"

"Merrick and Siani are safe. Merrick brought me here to help him look for you while he keeps Gower busy." She focused on the timber of the door she was pressed against and the metal handle she clutched. It barely helped.

"Gower? My brother-in-law?"

Before Audrey could say anything else, footsteps on the stairs had her turning to face the other end of the hallway. Two simply dressed humans stepped into the hallway. They stared at Audrey, unmoving. She stared back at them, having no idea what to do.

"Are you still there?" Tanwen asked.

The older one pushed past the younger one. "You chose the wrong direction when you decided to run today."

She couldn't very well tell the woman she'd

actually chosen the correct one. Especially since she hadn't been running. "You could let me go. No one has to know I was here."

"I'm not about to be punished for letting you go," the younger woman said. "No one ever helped me when I ran."

The older woman gave the younger one a look. "Hush. Go tell the guards we found her." She waited until the younger woman had left before she spoke, moving close and lowering her voice. "I'll try and ensure they don't chain you so you have a chance to escape. Run south. Eventually, you'll reach the Fringes. Wait until just on dawn as there are wolves in the forest."

"Why would you do this?"

"I tried to run once." The woman touched the cluster of keys hanging from her belt. "It seems a shame Tanwen can't go with you." She fiddled with one of the shorter keys. "But there are only a few keys that can open her chains." She let the key go.

Audrey stared at her. Was the woman trying to tell her something? She was close enough that she could reach out and grab the key, but the woman would realise.

The woman glanced over her shoulder. "I don't know what's taking them so long." She unhooked the keys and used them to unlock the door, half opening it. "You can go in here." She grabbed Audrey's arm when she started to enter the room, keeping her voice low. "Don't cross Gower. He's not an enemy worth having." She spun from Audrey at a sound. "About time. I don't have all day. I have other work that needs to be done."

Audrey looked from the woman's back to the keys hanging in the door, unable to see anything past the woman. It didn't take her long to come to a decision and she slipped the key off the hoop, pocketing it before she stepped further into the room. She met Tanwen's gaze, looking away when she saw the hope in the Fae's eyes. She didn't want to risk giving away their plan to escape, to whoever was in the hallway.

The door swung fully open and two warriors stepped in with the woman. The taller one looked Audrey up and down. "She doesn't seem like much for all the fuss she's caused."

The woman held onto the edge of the door. "Leave her here until her master is gone and we find out what our master wants done with her."

The warrior took a step towards the woman. "It's lord to you."

The woman shrugged. "What more can he do? There's no one left he can take from me."

Audrey wished she could do something to help the woman. Anger raced through her. Who did Gower think he was? The anger was quickly followed by frustration. She was as powerless as both Tanwen and the woman. It took a great deal of effort not to touch the key she'd shoved in a pocket. Soon she'd be out of here.

The taller warrior turned to the other one. "Fetch a chain and we'll put her beside this one." He nodded towards Tanwen.

"How do you think she'll get out of here?" The woman gestured towards the window. "Turn into a bird and fly through that?"

The warrior looked between Audrey and the window several times before he strode from the room. "Lock the door."

Audrey mouthed the words 'thank you' when only the woman was in the room with them.

The woman nodded and closed the door. The clunk of it locking was loud in the room.

Chapter Sixteen

Audrey waited until it was silent before she moved closer to Tanwen. "I don't know how long we have until Gower decides what to do with me." She looked over the Fae, relieved to see she appeared reasonably unharmed. Apart from looking ill. Hopefully, she should be able to escape with her. What did surprise her was how young the Fae looked. As young as Merrick. She had the same dark hair and eyes as Merrick and her hair was pulled back from her narrow face, showing her slightly pointed ears. The Fae did not look like she was sixty-eight.

Tanwen held out her hands, magic forming in them. "Take it from me. I can't last long with these iron chains and all my magic. Not unless my brother arrives in the next few minutes."

A light perfume filled the air, one that reminded Audrey of spring. She drew out the key, grinning. "I have something better." She guessed Tanwen hadn't been able to see her take the key with the angle the door had been on.

"You have the key?" The magic sank back into Tanwen's hands.

Nodding, Audrey held the chain in place so she could unlock the padlock. "Yeah, but I'm not sure how we're going to get out of this room. I can't exactly turn into a bird and fly out the window." She lowered the chains to the floor, not wanting to make too much noise by letting them fall. "And Merrick doesn't exactly know where I am. I'd planned to meet up with him."

Tanwen formed a bright green leaf, the colour of one newly formed. "I can take us out of here." The light scent of her magic again filled the air.

"You can travel with magic like your brother can?"

"Most Fae are capable of that." Tanwen took hold of Audrey's arm. "Where are we to meet Merrick?"

"Uhm, we never sorted that out."

"Then I'm going home."

Before Audrey could protest about leaving Merrick behind, the world shimmered and reformed. They were in a spacious bedroom, Siani and Jordan sitting on the end of the bed, his arm around her.

Siani jumped up at the sight of them, running

forward to throw her arms around Tanwen. "I was terrified they'd killed you."

After hugging her close, Tanwen held Siani at arm's length. "Who is the human and what is going on here?"

Audrey moved closer to Jordan. "My brother. And I'm sure he was only comforting your daughter." She gave her brother a look to let him know that better have been all he was doing.

Siani pulled away from her mother, smiling at her. "This is Jordan. He doesn't live in this realm. You should hear what his realm is like."

"No. Not until you're eighteen," Tanwen stated.

"Mother." Siani filled the word with exasperation and pleading. "It's not that bad. Jordan can show me around."

Audrey nearly groaned when she saw the look Tanwen gave her brother. She needed Merrick here. But they'd left him behind. It dawned on her that she had a way of contacting him. Taking the leaf out of her pocket, she brought it to her lips. "We've returned to the castle." She lowered it. "Whereabouts in the castle are we exactly?"

Tanwen broke off from the argument she was having with Siani. "My bedroom." She turned back to her daughter. "Your gratefulness at finding me alive didn't last long."

Audrey raised the leaf to her lips again. "We're in your sister's bedroom."

Seconds later, there was a knock on Tanwen's door. She broke off mid-argument with Siani, who was determined to return with Jordan to see his world. Tanwen swung the door open. "You escaped the trap?"

Merrick shook his head. "Audrey rescued me."

Tanwen remained in the doorway, turning to face Audrey. "It seems we both owe you a debt for that." She paused a moment. "How do you want us to repay you?"

Audrey didn't hesitate. "I need to find and rescue my parents."

"I'm working on that," Merrick said.

"Surely there's something we can do in the meantime," Audrey said.

"Whatever it is you're working on, I want to help," Jordan said.

"I want to help too," Siani added.

Tanwen faced her daughter. "You need to go somewhere safe until Gower is no longer a threat."

Audrey wished she could say the same thing to her brother. A smile nearly escaped. "What if she stays with Jordan at our place in Brisbane? No one would be able to find her there. No one knows who we are."

"No," Tanwen said.

Merrick slowly nodded. "It might be the best place for her. We can send a knight with them."

"What about iron sickness?" Tanwen asked.

"We won't leave her there forever." Merrick moved further into the room, standing in front of his sister. "Do you plan to let him get away with this?"

"No. I didn't know he was behind the attack until Audrey told me, but that changes nothing. The servants and guards who attended me weren't ones I'd seen on any of my visits to his home, not that I would have seen all those who serve him. If I'd been able to use my magic to leave, I never would have known who held me captive." Tanwen stepped around Merrick, placing her hand on Siani's shoulder. "You will listen to whichever knight I send with you."

"I'm going to the human realm?" Siani asked.

Tanwen pointed her forefinger at Siani. "Wipe that expression off your face. It will not be for fun. You're going for your protection."

Audrey wished she could say something to her brother. Warn him about getting too close to Siani and demand to know what he'd been doing earlier.

But she couldn't do that with the Fae's mother and uncle standing with them. "How will you be able to take her there? And my brother will need Fae food."

"As long as he can picture the place clearly, one of our knights can take them both there." Tanwen nodded towards Jordan.

"I can," Jordan said.

"Then I'll organise it immediately. Along with food." Tanwen strode from her bedroom, beckoning her daughter to follow.

Siani left with a glance over her shoulder and a smile for Jordan.

Audrey nearly sighed heavily. That was all she needed. More problems.

"I'll see if my knights are back." Merrick left them in Tanwen's room.

Audrey waited a moment before moving close to her brother. "What were you thinking? You better not go causing any more problems. Don't you understand she won't be able to stay in our world?"

"Who says I want to stay in our world?" Jordan asked.

"But..." Audrey's voice trailed off as she tried to think of a reason why he had to remain in their world. "What about the rest of us? Are you going to stay here without us?"

"You could stay here too. I bet you could ask for anything. You've saved two of them," Jordan said. "Look around you. Isn't this place amazing?"

She did a slow turn, taking in the opulent surroundings. She'd barely had time to do more than keep trying to find a way to rescue all of them. "Yeah, but humans aren't considered very important in the realms of the Fae."

"Humans with magic are," Jordan said. "Or at least they are in this place. You were right. Not all Fae are the same."

"You're going to get magic?" Audrey asked.

Jordan grinned. "No point in not having any if I decide to stay here."

"What about Mum and Dad? I doubt they'd let you stay."

Jordan's grin remained in place. "I doubt they'd be able to stop me."

A sound had Audrey facing the door. It was a human servant. She couldn't help noticing how much better dressed the servants were here and that made her think of the woman who'd helped them. If anyone was owed a debt, it was certainly her.

The servant faced Jordan. "They are waiting for you, sir."

Jordan grinned, glancing at Audrey. "See. Isn't it amazing here?"

She was tempted to roll her eyes. Instead, she placed a hand on her brother's arm. "Be careful." She wanted to remind him of her earlier words. But she couldn't. Not with the servant standing in front of them, waiting.

He grinned again. "Stop worrying about me." His expression sobered. "You're the one who will be in danger. You make sure you take care." He hesitated a moment. "Do you think you'll be able to find them?"

She knew exactly who he was talking about. She was terrified something would happen before she could find their dad and rescue him and their mum. "I won't stop looking until I do. And I'll bring both of them home."

Nodding, Jordan turned and followed the servant from the room.

Watching him leave, Audrey felt alone. There were very few people she knew in this realm and even less that she trusted. Closing her eyes, she tried not to think of everything that might go wrong. There were a lot of things that could end in disaster. Opening her eyes, she found Merrick standing in front of her, concern in his eyes.

"Are you hurt?"

She shook her head.

He closed the small amount of distance between them, running his fingers across her cheek and towards her hair. "You could wait here."

"No." She didn't have to think about it. "You're not leaving me behind." Even though she dreaded to think what they might face.

Merrick smiled. "All right. I won't leave you behind."

"What do we need to do first?"

"Sayer learned about a Demi Fae, Idris, who has a score to settle with Madlen. We're going to visit him and see if he can give us any information that will help us figure out where she might be keeping your father," Merrick said.

"When?"

"Now if you wish."

She grinned. "Did you really think I'd want to wait?"

Merrick chuckled softly, holding out his hand. "No." He formed an autumn leaf in his other hand.

Audrey stared at the leaf. The curling around the edges was getting worse. "What happens when the leaf is completely dead?"

"It won't get that far." He continued to hold out his hand. "I've never heard of that happening."

Chapter Seventeen

Audrey placed her hand in Merrick's, wanting to ask more questions about the leaf. Meeting his gaze, she saw the wild look was back in them. Before she could ask him if he was okay, he crushed the leaf and the world shimmered around them, reforming as a narrow alleyway. "Where are we?" She kept hold of his hand, not liking the look of the dingy area he'd brought her to, the dilapidated buildings pressing in on her. Peering upwards, she caught a glimpse of the sky, focusing on it rather than the cramped space.

"This way." His words were clipped as he tugged her along the alleyway, stopping at the end to look both ways onto a cobblestone street that was rutted and missing many of the cobblestones, weeds growing amongst them.

"Where are we going?" She remained close to him, eyeing the figures huddled together on the other side of the road, pressed against buildings that looked like they might fall apart at any minute.

Merrick didn't answer, drawing her around the corner with him to stop in front of a worn, timber door. He rapped sharply on it.

Peering around them, Audrey half wished they'd remained in the alleyway. It had to be bad when she wanted to remain in a cramped space. But it felt like everyone watched them and most of those doing the watching were hidden. A shiver ran down her spine and she moved closer to Merrick, her body pressed against the warmth of his.

The door swung open and a young man glared at them. "What do you want?"

Audrey nearly stared open-mouthed at him, managing to press her lips tightly together instead. His pale hair was in a tangled mess around his face, reaching all the way to his waist. His clothes looked like they were little more than rags, he clutched a dagger in one hand and he smelled like he hadn't washed in months. Looked like it as well. It wasn't any of these that made her want to stand there gaping. It was the wild look in his pale brown, almost golden, eyes. It reminded her of the look Merrick currently had.

"Revenge against Madlen," Merrick said. "She has

something of ours and we need to find out where it might be hidden."

Idris grinned, his teeth appearing to have been filed to a point. "Come on in." He stepped to the side, gesturing them inside with the hand that clutched the dagger. "Is it something she values greatly?"

Merrick entered the dwelling. "She values it far more than I do." Merrick shrugged. "But I'm not about to give her the satisfaction of keeping something she stole."

Idris chuckled. "No, no." He shook his head. "Never give her any satisfaction in life. Don't give her death either. She must suffer."

Audrey wanted to step back from Idris when he came close, peering into their faces. She was tempted to step behind Merrick rather than remain at his side, but his warning about letting others know her fears kept her in place.

"Big or little. What is the object? She has places. Many places." Idris nodded, chuckling again. "I know all her hidey holes. She sends her people after me, but I'm too cunning for them." He made a slashing motion with his dagger. "Too fast."

Audrey's gaze followed the movement of the dagger. What was wrong with him? How had he ended up like this?

"She thought she could play her games with me. I'll be the one who plays the games." Idris pointed at them with the dagger. "You hear me?" His voice rose.

Merrick drew away from Audrey, putting himself between her and Idris. "Then tell us where her hidey holes are. And we'll help you play your games."

"Why would you help me? What's in it for you?" Idris demanded.

"Making sure she doesn't win."

Idris backed away from Merrick, bringing the dagger up. "You stay away from me. You're one of her games too. I see it in your eyes."

"Tell me what I want to know and we'll be gone." Merrick took a step towards Idris.

Audrey wanted to run. Wanted to leave this crazy place and never return. But that wouldn't help her free her parents. She stepped to the side so she could see Idris more clearly. "What games? And what do you see in his eyes?"

Idris looked between the two of them, his movements jerky as he eased around the room to come closer to Audrey. "You're not one of hers." He stared into her eyes, pointing towards Merrick with the dagger. "He is. You better watch him. Her games end in death." He peered into her face, his face overly close. "You want to die?"

She wanted to back away from him. The smell she could have tolerated. It was the look in his eyes and the dagger in his hand that had her wanting to retreat. Somehow she managed to hold her ground. "You lived through them."

"Are you sure?" He cackled. "Are you really sure of that?"

She hadn't been sure of anything for days. "Then what are you if not alive?"

"That is the question." He slowly nodded his head. "That is the question she never answers. The games continue and the bodies pile up." He frowned, taking a step back from her. "Who are you? What are you doing here?" A look of confusion swept over his face, the wild look momentarily vanishing.

"You were going to tell us where to find the things Madlen doesn't want found." Merrick grabbed hold of Idris' arm, twisting it until the dagger fell to the floor. "Now where are they?"

"Merrick, let-" Audrey broke off when she saw the wild look in his eyes. It was worse than Idris' had been. She backed away from him. "Merrick?" She glanced between the two males and the exit. There was no way she could get past either of them to reach it.

Idris wrenched himself from Merrick's grip when

Audrey distracted him, scooping up the dagger before scurrying across the room. He slipped behind Audrey, grabbing hold of her shoulder and using her as a shield. "She sent you. I know she did. I know her games."

Audrey froze, catching glimpses of the dagger when Idris used it for emphasis, regularly pointing it at Merrick. "She has someone I want to free." Idris stilled, his breathing loud in her ear. She didn't know what to say next. Had no idea how this world worked. She could only guess at what was going on. "How did you escape from her?"

Idris spun her to face him, his arm around her, keeping her close. "She knows. She knows the answer to that question."

It took all her self-control not to move. Not to break free from his grip and put as much space between them as possible. The look of confusion was back on his face, the wild look gone again. "She might know, but I don't. How did you escape?"

"She thought me dead." He cackled, the wild look returning. "I fooled her. Thought me dead and threw me out for the wolves. Didn't want my corpse stinking up her place. Not that it would have mattered. The place always stinks of death." He put his face close, his gaze meeting hers. "You don't have the look of death." He jerked his head away, glancing in Merrick's direction. "He does. It won't be long now." He grinned.

A shudder went through her at seeing the pointed teeth so close. "What won't be long?"

"I've outlasted them all. The first to play the game and the last to survive. She doesn't know what she's doing. Only makes it worse. We aren't meant to live amongst humans. This is our realm. She brought the death back with her."

She wanted to shake him. Wanted to tell him to make sense. "Where did you escape from?"

He cackled, sheathing the dagger in the leather sheath that hung at his side. "You want to see death?" He formed a pebble, the scent of his magic overpowered by the smell of metal. "Come visit death with me."

Before Audrey could decline, he grabbed hold of her arm.

Merrick threw himself at the two of them, grabbing hold of Idris as the world shimmered and reformed around them. His momentum forced the three of them against the trunk of a broad tree, breaking them apart. Audrey tried to gain her balance, ending up sprawled on the ground, winded from the collision with the tree.

Idris backed away, drawing his dagger again. "I knew it. You're from her." He formed another pebble, vanishing from view.

Audrey, still sprawled on the ground, stared up at Merrick. "What do we do now?" She would have preferred to yell at him for scaring off the one person who might help her find her dad. It was close, but the look in his eyes had her warily watching him, not daring to move in case she startled him.

Merrick stood above her, staring down at her, the wild look remaining in his eyes.

"Merrick?" She spoke his name softly, wanting to get up off the ground.

He blinked several times then held out his hand. "Are you unharmed?"

She let him draw her to her feet. "Yeah." She examined his face. "Are you okay?"

A look of confusion momentarily crossed his face. He glanced around the area. "We need to figure out why he brought us here." He kept hold of her hand, walking off in the direction he faced.

She stumbled on the rough ground, his grip keeping her upright. "Merrick? What happened?"

He glanced at her, remaining silent.

"Answer me. Please." She tugged on his hand, wanting him to stop and talk to her. "Will you end up like him? He escaped from Madlen too. What is she doing to people?" She drew in a sharp breath. "What about my parents? Will they end up like Idris?"

"Look around. There has to be something around here." Merrick changed directions. "He brought us here for a reason. One related to Madlen."

She wanted to growl in frustration. Instead, she did as he said. She still needed to find her dad. That hadn't changed. But she also needed to figure out what was going on with Merrick. Was this normal or had Madlen done something to him?

Merrick changed directions again and Audrey realised they were doing ever widening circles from the point where Idris had left them. "What made Idris a Demi Fae rather than a Fae? He looked like a Fae to me." He'd had the typical pointy ears.

"Mixed race. One parent was a Light Fae while the other was a Wood Fae."

"But doesn't that just make him Fae?"

Merrick glanced at her, the wild look completely gone from his eyes. "Don't you differentiate between the races in your world?"

She started to say that the races in her world weren't as varied as the ones in his when she caught a glimpse of a house through the trees. "Is that what we're looking for?" She pointed it out when Merrick looked in the wrong direction.

He picked up his pace, heading directly towards the house. "It might be."

She tugged on his hand. "Slow down. I'm not used to traipsing around forests like this."

He slowed a little, but still kept up a steady pace, not slowing until they reached the edge of the tree line. "The place looks deserted."

Chapter Eighteen

Audrey's heart sank. Had they risked their lives for nothing? She thought of the dagger and the wild look in Idris' eyes. She was amazed he hadn't stabbed either of them. Actually, she was amazed Merrick hadn't attacked him with the way he'd been behaving. She glanced at Merrick, relieved his eyes remained clear. "Are we going to check it out anyway?"

Merrick inclined his head. "Things are not always as they seem in this realm."

"No kidding," she muttered under her breath.

Merrick glanced at her. A grin fleetingly appeared. He took several steps towards the house, glancing at her once more. "Did you want to wait here?"

"Not likely." She moved closer to him. The day was getting later and she had no doubt there were wolves in the forest. "You're not leaving me behind."

Merrick gestured to the left. "We'll circle around

and see what's behind the house. No point striding into a trap if that is all it is."

She remained at his side, his hand still holding hers. She frequently glanced at her hand in his. The last person she'd held hands with had been a boyfriend. It seemed odd to be holding Merrick's hand. Not that she pulled away from him. As odd as it felt, it was also comforting. Her gaze was drawn upwards from their hands. She'd never met anyone in her world as gorgeous and interesting as Merrick.

He looked towards her, slowing when their gazes met. "Is something wrong?"

She wondered what he saw in her gaze to ask that question. Shaking her head, she looked away, focusing on the house instead. "What if my dad isn't in there?" The timber house was two storeys high, had curtains drawn at all the windows and was set in rambling gardens that were overgrown.

"We visit Idris again."

She wanted to protest, but was beginning to realise there was very little she wasn't willing to do to find her family. The stairs in the basement came to mind. Okay, there were a couple of things, but there weren't many.

They approached the rear of the house, discovering all the windows had bars on them and the back door was locked. Merrick stepped back from the door and looked upwards. "I can't use magic to travel inside unless I know what it looks like."

"Then we find a window that doesn't have a curtain." She tugged him across the back of the house to the next window. It was completely closed. Stepping back and looking upwards showed the window above had a drawn curtain. Straightening her shoulders, she refused to give in to the feeling of hopelessness that washed over her. Surely they'd be able to find some way inside.

It wasn't until they were halfway across the side of the house that they found a curtain that wasn't fully drawn. Audrey grinned at Merrick. "Is that what you need?"

Merrick formed an autumn leaf, tightening his grip on her hand as he peered through the gap in the curtain. The world shimmered around them and they were inside when it reformed.

Audrey scanned the room, a couple of pieces of dusty furniture haphazardly scattered across the timber floor. "It's like they were disturbed partway through moving out."

Merrick took a step forward, letting go of her hand to draw his sword. "They haven't left." He strode from the room.

She hurried after him. "What are you planning to do?" Coming alongside him, she caught a glimpse of his eyes. The dim interior of the house wasn't dark enough to hide the wildness in them. "Merrick."

He kept moving, not even glancing at her.

"Stop. Please." She had no idea what he planned to do, but that look in his eyes didn't bode well. She grabbed hold of his left arm, trying to tug him to a stop.

He turned to face her. Anger was mixed with the wild look in his eyes. "What do you think you're doing?"

She kept hold of him, stepping close so he wouldn't have room to swing his sword. Or at least she hoped he wouldn't. Continuing to meet his gaze, she clung to his arm when he tried to draw away from her. "You said you'd never hurt me." Her words were soft and at first, she didn't think he heard.

Confusion momentarily filled his eyes, replaced by the wild look. "Then let me go. I can hear them upstairs. I have to catch them before they escape."

"Not like this, Merrick. You remind me of Idris."

The wild look faltered, returning just as strong. "I am nothing like him."

She hesitated, not sure how far gone he was. And he was gone. The wild look seemed to have overwhelmed what she normally saw in his eyes, as if another person peered through them at her. "Who are you?"

He frowned. "What kind of question is that?"

"Who are you?" Was there such a thing as possession? She had no idea what existed in the world. Obviously. She hadn't even known of the existence of Fae. How many other fantastical things were real?

The wild look faltered again.

She pressed her other hand against his heart, keeping hold of his arm as she came close enough that there was barely any space between them. "Who are you?"

The wild look was replaced by confusion. "Audrey?" Sheathing his sword, he tentatively ran his fingers down the side of her face.

"What happened to you?"

He didn't answer, only continued to lightly touch her face, his gaze tracing the same path. When his gaze met hers, his fingers stilled. "I'll return you to my parents' estate. It's not safe for you to remain with me."

She drew away from him when he formed an autumn leaf, a metallic scent lingering in the air, the wild look back in his eyes. "No. I'm not leaving you and you need to stop doing magic."

Merrick started towards her, his hand reaching for his sword. Before he could draw it, a man ran at him, leaping on his back. Merrick threw himself against the wall, trying to dislodge the man.

It took Audrey a few seconds to realise she recognised Merrick's attacker. "No! Don't hurt him. That's my dad."

Fred fell to the floor, leaping to his feet in a fluid movement.

Merrick drew his sword, the autumn leaf fluttering to the floor. He drew back his weapon.

Audrey threw herself at Fred, trying to hold him back. "Dad. Dad! It's me, Dad." His body felt thinner than usual and his clothes were ripped and dirty. "Dad." Her words made no difference. "Fred." Even his name didn't sink in. Tears welled in her eyes as Fred escaped her grip, launching himself at Merrick.

She spun, throwing herself at Merrick too, her hand slamming against his arm to prevent the sword from reaching Fred. "Merrick. That's my dad. You can't hurt him. Please. We have to take him from here."

Running footsteps headed towards them as Fred collided with Merrick, knocking Audrey to the floor.

She landed by the autumn leaf. Snatching it up, she scrambled to her feet, looking from the direction of the oncoming footsteps and the two who were fighting. From the approaching noise, there had to be more than one person headed their way.

The sword was knocked from Merrick's hand as he fought to escape Fred's grip.

Audrey scooped up the sword, running towards the two. "Take me to your parents' estate." She held out the leaf, meeting Merrick's gaze as he wrestled with her dad. "Now."

A moment of clarity formed in Merrick's eyes and he broke free from Fred's grip long enough to snatch the leaf and take the sword, sheathing it before he grabbed hold of her hand.

She wasn't about to leave her dad behind. Jerking Merrick forward, she grabbed hold of Fred's arm as he struggled to rise from the floor where he'd fallen when Merrick had escaped him. The world shimmered and reformed, bringing them to the dining room of the castle.

Fred broke free from her grip, knocking her to the floor as he again attacked Merrick who tried to draw his sword. Merrick didn't have a chance. But that didn't stop him from attacking Fred, driving him across the room and into the wall, breaking free from his grip.

Audrey scrambled to her feet. "Help me. Someone,

help." She ran to the doorway, peering into the hallway. Two Fae ran towards her, their footsteps silent. She only recognised one of them. Luw. "Don't hurt either of them." She stepped out of the doorway.

The two Fae subdued Fred, leaving Merrick loose. He drew his sword.

Audrey stepped in front of him, fear racing through her at the look in his eyes. "Merrick. No. Please don't. That's my dad."

Merrick brushed her aside.

She grabbed hold of his arm. "Please." Stepping in front of him again, she threw her arms around him, looking up at him as she held on tight. "Merrick. Please."

He faltered, looking down at her.

She tightened her arms around him. "Whatever she's done to you, fight it. Don't let her win."

"What is wrong with him?" Luw asked.

"Put my dad somewhere safe. Anywhere other than here with Merrick." She glanced over her shoulder, regretting the action when Merrick tried to break free from her grip again. She clung to him, relieved the two Fae vanished from the room, taking her dad with them.

"Unhand me." Merrick tried to pry her arms from around him with his free hand.

She had no idea what to do if he used the sword against her. Before she had the chance to find out if she could bring Merrick back, Luw and the other Fae returned, taking Merrick from her and vanishing. She stared at where they'd been, now alone in the room.

She staggered to the closest chair, dropping onto it hard. She had no idea what to do. Her dad was crazy, her mum needed to be rescued, Merrick wasn't himself and her brother needed to regularly eat Fae food. She dropped her head into her hands, certain there were probably other things she was forgetting. How had things become so out of control?

"Can I help you?"

Raising her head from her hands, Audrey met Luw's gaze. "I need to get my mum." She stood up. "What did you do with Merrick?"

"He will sleep for now."

"That doesn't tell me what you did with him. And my dad. Where is he? Can I see him? And I want to see Merrick too."

"Which do you want to do first?" Luw asked.

She didn't have a clue. Everything. All at once. But that wasn't possible. At least not as far as she knew. "I want to go with whoever goes after my mum. She might not let a stranger take her anywhere."

Luw inclined his head. "Is that what you wish to do first?"

She started to say yes, but who knew how long she'd be gone. Not with how time worked between here and her world. "I want to see my dad, then Merrick and then we can go."

Luw held out his hand. "I'll take you to your father. But I can't let you near him. He's dangerous."

Chapter Nineteen

Audrey wanted to protest that her dad would never hurt her. The words remained unspoken and she placed her hand in Luw's. "Thank you." The moment she took Luw's hand, the world shimmered and reformed and she found herself staring at the barred window of a dungeon door. "You shoved him in a dungeon?" She turned to Luw. "Get him out of there."

"If he hurts someone, I can't guarantee his safety," Luw said.

"But a dungeon?" She peered between the bars. There was a lantern hanging from the ceiling, casting a soft light across the floor of the dungeon. It was bright enough she could see her dad prowl the area, regularly throwing himself against the walls as if he could escape that way. He threw himself at the door and she jumped back. "What happened to his wrists?"

They were raw and bloody and she wanted to do something about them. Her gaze followed him as he continued to prowl the dungeon.

"He had iron bands around each wrist. We removed them," Luw said.

"Iron bands? Why would they make such a mess of his wrists?"

"He has Fae magic."

She glanced at Luw before returning to staring at her dad. "How did he end up with Fae magic?"

"He isn't exactly in a state of mind to ask," Luw said.

She nearly didn't ask, was afraid of the answer. She forced herself to speak. "Is there a way to cure him?"

"What are you wanting to cure?"

"His madness."

Luw shrugged. "That would depend on what has been done to him."

"How do I find out?"

"Usually the easiest way is to ask the person who did it."

"What if that isn't an option?"

Luw shrugged again.

She wanted to demand he tell her something. Anything. Instead, she drew in a deep breath, trying to remain calm. "Can you take me to see Merrick?"

Luw held out a hand.

She placed hers in his, the world reforming around her, the scent of his magic hanging in the air. The shock of seeing Merrick stretched out on a bed, his eyes closed, had her holding onto Luw's hand longer than necessary. She let it go, stepping away from him. "Will he be okay?" She couldn't bring herself to move forward and check on Merrick for fear of what she might find. When Luw didn't answer, she looked towards him.

He shrugged.

"How can you not know?"

"He was told it is iron sickness. Yet it hasn't continued to behave like iron sickness."

"Who would know?"

He gave her a look.

It made her want to growl in frustration. "Other than the person who caused it."

"Going to the source is always the best option," Luw said.

Turning her back on Luw, she finally managed to cross the space between her and Merrick. She sat on the edge of his bed, running her fingers across his forehead. He felt warm, but not hot. She frowned. Were Fae the same temperature as humans?

"Are you ready to leave now?" Luw asked.

Mentally promising Merrick that she'd find out what had been done to him, she rose to her feet. "We need to take another Fae with us. One who can help transport the other prisoners out of there."

Luw inclined his head. "I'll collect Sayer then return for you." He left the room through the door, closing it behind him.

Audrey looked from the door to Merrick, not sure what she should do. She sat beside him again, taking his hand in hers. "I will find out what she did to you."

Merrick's eyes slowly opened and he blinked several times. "Audrey?" A frown formed. "Where am I?"

She could only guess at the location. "In your bedroom." It seemed like a logical enough answer since why would they have put him in someone else's room.

He tried to sit up.

She pressed a hand against his chest. "Sleep."

"I have to help you rescue your mother."

She continued to press her hand against his chest. "That's all sorted."

"She's been rescued?"

She didn't want to lie to him, but also didn't want to tell him the truth and have him think he needed to get out of bed. "Luw and Sayer are taking care of it."

He relaxed back against the bed, a smile forming. "They'll bring her back safely." His eyes closed. "They've never failed me before."

She was tempted to point out they'd let his sister be captured. Pressing her lips together, she remained silent. He needed to sleep. Not worry about what would happen when she went with Luw and Sayer to Madlen's basement. Letting go of his hand, she eased away from him, rising to her feet. When he remained motionless, she backed away to the door, slipping into the hallway to wait for the knights.

The two of them strode towards her, stopping in front of her, each holding out a hand. The moment she took hold of their hands, Luw transported them to the basement. She knew it was him by the scent of his magic. The moment they arrived, she ran towards the cage her mum had been in last time she was here. She held onto the cage bars, peering inside. For a moment she thought the cage was empty. Then the bundle of rags shifted and she realised it was her mum. She drew in a sharp breath.

Luw shifted her out of the way, using the same crystal as last time to unlock the cage. He handed the crystal to Sayer. "Unlock the rest of the cages before someone comes down here." Luw picked up Joan, slinging her over his shoulder before turning to

Audrey and holding out his hand. "I'll take the two of you back to the castle."

Audrey took a step back. That wouldn't help her learn what had happened to Merrick. "Take one of the prisoners first. Come back for me. You won't be able to take all of them with you in a single trip, anyway."

Luw nodded, picking up one of the other prisoners and throwing her over his other shoulder. He vanished seconds later, leaving behind only the scent of his magic, Sayer also leaving.

Audrey hurried up the stairs, testing the door. Relief rushed through her at finding it unlocked. She'd half expected it to be locked. Slowly turning the handle, she eased the door open, peering through the gap. The kitchen appeared empty so she slipped through the doorway, closing the door behind her as she scanned the room. She was alone.

The kitchen was lit with the early light of dawn. Her heart leapt. Surely Madlen didn't sleep with her notes. Not that she knew where the Fae slept, but supposed she better start looking if she had any hope of finding out.

She went from room to room, methodically searching downstairs. The room Merrick had been held in remained empty, as were the rest of the rooms.

She paused at the bottom of the stairs, looking up them. The house remained silent. Although she doubted it'd stay that way. Sooner or later one or both of them would rise for the morning.

Creeping up the stairs, she winced when one of the treads made a noise. Freezing in place, she held her breath as she listened for Madlen and the nephew. Nothing seemed to stir. Slowly letting out her breath, she continued up the stairs. Reaching the top, she looked in both directions. Still nothing moved and everything remained silent.

She had no idea how much time she had until Luw returned for her and the last prisoner. Or how long until Madlen woke. With how the morning continued to brighten, she had to assume she didn't have much longer. Possibly not enough time to search both directions. Yet she had no idea which one to search first.

Going left, she hoped she wouldn't regret the choice. She crept along the hallway to the last room, peeking inside. Her heart felt like it stopped when she spotted Madlen asleep in the bed, the curtains not fully drawn so that a beam of sunlight slowly crept across the floor towards the bed.

A glance around the room showed nothing that looked like it might be used to store notes. She momentarily closed her eyes, opening them to stare at the lengthening beam of light. Standing around wasn't going to help. It'd only get her caught. Although there was a good chance entering the room would get her caught too. She stepped inside the room anyway. She wouldn't learn anything by remaining in the hallway.

She placed one foot in front of the other, testing the surface before she put weight on it. The floorboards remained silent. Step by step she came closer to Madlen, her gaze not leaving the Fae as she watched her carefully, ready to run if she woke. Reaching the side of the bed, her gaze roamed the area, trying to spot anything that could help. About to turn away, she spotted the corner of a leather bound book poking out from underneath the pillow. Fighting back disappointment, she momentarily closed her eyes. Opening them made no difference. The book remained under the pillow and Madlen's head was in the middle of the pillow.

She tried to figure out the size of the book from what she could see, her gaze drawn from Madlen's head to the edge of the book. Depending on the size of it, the Fae might not actually have her head on top of the book.

Crouching beside the bed, she reached for the

book, her fingers closing over the edge. She tugged slightly, pausing to stare at Madlen. The Fae didn't move, nor was there a change in her breathing.

Audrey drew the book slowly out from beneath the pillow, going light headed from holding her breath so long. Pausing, she breathed in and out several times before continuing, afraid Madlen would wake at any minute. When the book was completely out from underneath the pillow, she had to hold herself still at the rush of relief and excitement that washed over her. She'd done it. She eased back from the bed, clutching the book to her chest, wishing she had something to carry it in.

Far enough from the bed, she rose to her feet and turned to face the door, taking a step towards it. A noise had her freezing and looking over her shoulder at Madlen.

The Fae rolled over, her hand slipping beneath the pillow. She was awake instantly.

Audrey didn't wait around to see what she'd do. She raced for the door and stepped into the hallway.

"Nephew!" Madlen called out.

Chapter Twenty

Seeing a door open up further down the hallway, Audrey slipped into the room next to Madlen's frantically scanning the area. There was no key to lock the door and someone was likely to burst in at any moment. Spotting a large chest of drawers, she pushed them across in front of the door. It wouldn't keep anyone out for long, but hopefully it'd give her enough time to escape. She ran to the window and drew back the curtain, opening the window. It would take her too long to climb down and the nephew would catch her

A glance around showed only a wardrobe and underneath the bed as potential hiding places. Leaving the curtain drawn open, she slipped under the bed, huddling against the wall under the middle of the bed, barely getting settled before the door was opening. The chest of drawers scraped across the floor.

The nephew burst into the room. "She's gone out the window."

Madlen followed him into the room. "Then go after her."

"Out the window?" The nephew took a step towards the window.

"Out the front door, you idiot," Madlen snapped. "Hurry. Before she escapes. She has my note journal."

The nephew raced from the room, Madlen following him. Audrey remained where she was, not daring to move. When the room remained silent, she peered out from underneath the bed, finding herself alone. She slipped out from under the bed, creeping to the doorway. Peering into the hallway, she saw Madlen was further along, remaining at the top of the stairs. It'd be impossible to get past her.

She looked from the journal to Madlen then back again. There was no way she could escape while carting the leather bound book around. Especially since it looked like the only escape was out the window.

Opening the journal she discovered approximately fifty pages had cramped handwriting covering them. Moving as far from the doorway as possible, she carefully tore out the pages, folding and hiding them in pockets and tucking them inside the waistband of her trousers. Grinning, she slid the journal under one of the pillows on the bed.

Crossing the room, she glanced towards the doorway before looking out the window. Both directions were clear. Audrey tried not to pay any attention to the thrill of excitement that ran through her. She might somehow pull this off.

She eased out the window, spotting her parents' car below. If she could make it to the car there was a key hidden under the rear of it due to how many times her dad had locked his keys in the car. Each time her mum had pointed out that if he had the central locking fixed it'd be impossible for him to leave them in the ignition.

If she could get the car started, which wasn't a definite with how little charge was in the battery, she could go home to Jordan and the two Fae who were with him. At least one of them should be able to return her to the realms of the Fae.

Reaching the edge of the roof, she peered over it in time to see the nephew go inside. Taking a deep breath, she tried to convince herself to jump. But the ground looked too far away. She slipped over the edge, clinging to it as she awkwardly dangled from the guttering. The metal creaked and she let go, bracing herself for the impact.

It wasn't as bad as she feared. Staggering, she immediately gained her balance, running lightly towards the car to crouch at the rear of it and run her hands underneath. It took her seconds to find the key, but it was too long. Before she reached the driver's door, the nephew was running towards her.

"Stop. Come back here or Madlen will make your family pay."

Her hands shook so hard she had no idea how she managed to unlock the door on the first attempt. Leaving it open, she sat in the seat, turning the key in the ignition. It made a laboured sound, not starting.

"Get out of the car," the nephew ordered.

Trying not to think about how close he was, she turned the key again. This time, it started and she put the vehicle into drive, slamming the door shut as she headed down the driveway. Her heart raced and she kept glancing in the rear view mirror at the nephew who followed, calling out after her. She had no idea where she was, but driving in any direction had to be better than remaining here.

It took an hour before she found a familiar location, a service station not far from the main highway. She pulled up, leaving the car running as she rested her head against the steering wheel, trying to stop shaking. She kept reminding herself she wasn't safe yet, that they might find her. Yet she couldn't stop shaking and didn't think she could safely drive until she had. Not that she really should be driving since all she had was a learner license.

The worry that they might somehow find her had Audrey continuing towards home well before she'd finished shaking. When she finally pulled up in front of their garage, she was exhausted and couldn't stop checking over her shoulder.

She sat where she was, the engine running and her head tilted back as she tried to figure out what to do next. What did she tell Jordan? Their mum looked like she hadn't eaten in a week, their dad had gone crazy and she had no idea if he'd ever be the same again. She closed her eyes, not wanting to go inside.

The sound of the garage door rolling upwards startled her and she stared at it as it rose. Her breath came out in a rush when she saw it was Jordan. She drove forward when he moved out of the way, turning off the engine once she was inside.

Jordan closed the roller door before coming to the driver's door and opening it. "Where are Mum and Dad?"

"In the realms of the Fae."

"You found them?" He leaned his arm against the top of the door.

She nodded, not sure how to tell him about them. "What day is it?"

"It's Sunday. We've been missing a week and a day."

She rose unsteadily from the car. "What do you mean by missing?"

"The police have been looking for us. You're lucky the neighbours are out." He gestured towards the right. "The nosey ones next door. They sent the police around here when we arrived on Friday. Fae magic works in this world too and they were able to hide us."

She closed the door of the car when her brother stepped back out of the way. "Who reported us missing?"

Jordan shrugged. "Could have been anyone. Mum and Dad didn't turn up at work last week. We didn't go to school." He shrugged again. "I have no idea how we'll explain any of this if we return here. It'd be easier to stay in the realms of the Fae."

She started to disagree with her brother, deciding she had more important things to deal with. "Where is the knight that brought you and Siani here?" She needed to return to the castle with Madlen's notes.

"In the lounge room." Jordan led the way.

Siani, who'd been curled up on the couch with a book, leapt to her feet. "How is my family? Has Gower been caught?"

Audrey shook her head. She turned to the knight who stood to the side of the window, his gaze regularly drawn to each of the possible entrances and the occupants. "I need you to take me to the castle."

"Until I've been relieved of duty, I cannot let Siani out of my sight."

"Why are you here?" Jordan asked Audrey.

Siani spoke almost at the same time as him. "I'm not some little child. I'm perfectly capable of looking after myself long enough for you to take her to our realm."

"Your mother says otherwise, as do your grandparents. I am to remain here with you," the knight stated.

"Will you stop treating me like a child?" Siani demanded. "You've hovered over me the entire time we've been here. You haven't let me go anywhere and you act like I'm about to be murdered at any second."

"Jordan will be here with her." Audrey said the words even though she knew by both his expression and tone that she was wasting her time. "I need to return to Merrick."

"I'm certain that if he wished me to leave his niece unattended to return you to him, he would have notified me. I haven't heard anything from any of the family." He stepped away from the wall. "Now if you will excuse me, I must do my patrol of the building." With a nod for each of them, he strode from the room.

She stared after him, his words eventually sinking in. Notify him. Why hadn't she thought of that already? She had the means to contact Merrick and let him know to collect her when he was awake. "I'm going to my room."

"Why?" Jordan asked.

She tried to think of a reason that wouldn't leave her brother worried about what was going to happen next. "I thought I should charge my phone. I'm sure there are a lot of messages from everyone."

"Mine is missing. Madlen probably has it," Jordan said.

She grinned at her brother. "It'll only be messages from Mike. You aren't missing anything." She strolled from the room chuckling at the uncomplimentary words her brother called out after her.

Once in her room, she closed the door and put her phone on to charge. Remaining standing, she took out the leaf, surprised it wasn't crushed into little pieces. She brought it to her lips. "I'm at my house with Jordan and Siani. I need someone to collect me and take me back to the castle. Can you tell the knight to take me back there? Or can you collect me when you're awake, Merrick?" A breeze came from nowhere and dragged the leaf from her fingers, swirling it around and behind the curtain.

She ran across the room, tugging the curtain partially aside in time to see the leaf somehow slip through the fly screen. She stared after it, open-mouthed. Letting the curtain fall back into place. Closing her mouth, she slowly shook her head. She should be accustomed to magic. But obviously, she wasn't.

Taking the pages of the journal out, she dropped onto the bed to read them while she waited. The handwriting was difficult to decipher at times and there were notes referring back and forth between the pages so that sometimes it was hard to make sense of everything and know which part of the experiment was most current. She was nearly finished reading the pages when a sentence had her sitting upright.

If Merrick continued to use his magic, he'd die. She stared at the words, reading them over several times. They didn't change. Hoping there was something further along in the notes about the discovery being incorrect, she read through the rest of the pages, rising to her feet as she did. It was impossible to sit still as she searched for a different answer.

There was none. She closed her eyes, swaying where she stood by the bed. She'd asked Merrick to come to her. Why hadn't she waited until after she'd read the pages? Although she'd also asked him to have the knight take her to the castle. There was a chance he'd do that.

Her heart sank. She doubted that very much. How many more times could Merrick use his magic without it killing him? She thought of the wild look in his eyes. Was that how Idris had survived? By not using his magic often? A knock on her door made her jump. She faced it.

"You still in there, Aude?" Jordan called out.

Chapter Twenty-One

Audrey gathered up the pages and shoved them in the top drawer of her desk. She didn't want her brother seeing them and worrying about what had been done to their parents. The last thing she needed was him trying to return to the realms of the Fae. He'd already been in enough danger. Slowing her breathing, she opened the door. "What's wrong?"

Jordan glanced past her before meeting her gaze. "Nothing. What have you been doing?"

She gestured to her bed. "Lying down." She had been. Earlier. That just hadn't been all she'd been doing.

"Oh." He glanced at the bed again. "Are you okay?"

She nodded.

He gestured in the direction he'd come from.

"Siani and I made lunch. It's only sandwiches. Did you know she's never prepared food before today?"

"She lives in a castle. What did you expect?"

"I don't know." He paused a moment. "Did you want to join us for lunch?"

She nodded. It had to be better than sitting around waiting to return to the realms of the Fae. "Sure."

Audrey found lunch more relaxing than she'd expected. Siani was entertaining and she was able to take her mind off the problems for a short while, even with the guard watching over them from one corner of the room. The moment she returned to her bedroom, they came crashing back in on her. Where was Merrick? Was he okay? Surely he wasn't still asleep.

She was the one who ended up falling asleep waiting for him. She woke to darkness and a noise in her room. Stretching out a hand, she turned on the bedside lamp. Merrick stood over her, a wild look in his eyes, his hand resting on the hilt of his sword. She didn't dare move, remaining stretched out towards the bedside cabinet.

"Why did you call me here?" Merrick demanded.

Her body began to tremble from being stretched out at such an awkward angle for so long. "To help you. But you shouldn't have come. When I called for you, I didn't know it would make you worse." She eased back slightly, not wanting to make any sudden movements. "How did you find your way here?"

"The leaf guided me." He frowned. "I know you?"

"Yes." She eased further away from the bedside cabinet. "I saved you." She didn't think it'd hurt to remind him.

His frown deepened. "You saved me?"

She slowly sat up, wanting to be on her feet rather than have him tower over her. "I saved you from Madlen." She took a small step to the side. "Do you remember being Madlen's prisoner?" She took another step. She wanted to glance at the door, but she didn't dare look away from him.

"Madlen." The word was almost a growl. He started to draw his sword from its scabbard.

She threw herself at him, trying to prevent him from drawing the sword. She had no idea what she'd do if he did. "She's not in here. It's just you and me."

He stilled, his gaze not leaving hers.

"Merrick?" She stared into his eyes, trying to see past the wild look.

His frown remained in place. "I know you." He sounded uncertain.

"Yes. You know me. I saved your life."

There was a sharp knock on the door. "Aude?" Jordan knocked on the door again.

Merrick pushed her aside, crossing the room in a blur of motion as he drew his sword and swung the door open.

Audrey staggered, barely remaining on her feet. "No." She raced after Merrick, putting herself between him and her brother. "Get out of here, Jordan."

"I'm not leaving you with-"

"Out of here, now, Jordan." She held Merrick's gaze, her hands held out to stop him and show she was unarmed.

"I will not-"

Merrick pushed Audrey aside again.

"No." She threw herself between them, pushing her brother back. A sharp pain had her drawing in her breath and she felt the sleeve of her shirt dampen.

"Audrey-"

She interrupted Jordan. "Get out of here now." She pressed her hand against her arm, drawing it away to see it was stained with blood.

"I'll get-" Jordan began.

"No." She barely glanced at her brother. "Just go." For a moment she thought she might have to tell him again, then she heard his footsteps retreating.

She continued to hold Merrick's gaze, seeing the confusion in his eyes.

Merrick's sword clattered to the floor, and he took a step forward, grabbing her hand to turn it towards him. "I hurt you." He reached for her arm. "I'll heal it."

"No." She drew back from him. "You can't. That's the problem." She could no longer see the wild look in his eyes. "What Madlen did to you, it'll kill you if you keep using your magic."

"I can never use it again?" Merrick demanded.

She shook her head. "Eventually. The length of time it took, for the two people who recovered, varied. But I don't know if it would have lasted because they tried to escape and she killed them."

He reached for her arm again. "One more time–"

"No." She brushed his hand aside. "You can't use it again until you're cured." She captured his hand when he reached for her again, clinging to it. "Please. It's barely a scratch." She tried to ignore the trickle of blood, hoping her sleeve hid it enough from his view. "Some tea-tree oil and a band aid will be enough."

"Merrick." Siani headed towards them along the hallway. "You're hurt?"

"No. Audrey is injured. She won't let me use my magic to heal her."

"Because it'll kill you." Audrey nearly yelled the words.

"How is that possible?" Siani asked.

"Madlen did something to him. I took her journal from her. Or at least the pages from her journal." She caught sight of her brother at the end of the hallway. She sent him a reassuring smile. It didn't remove the worry from his expression.

"Where are the pages?" Siani asked.

"She needs her arm seen to before she worries about any pages," Merrick said.

She let go of his hand, taking a step back. "Don't use your magic while I'm gone."

"Where are you going?" Merrick asked.

"The bathroom." She fled before he could follow. Once the door was closed, she rolled up her sleeve, momentarily closing her eyes at the amount of blood. She grabbed tissues from the box on the shelf that ran across the length of the mirror over the vanity, trying to clean up the mess. More blood welled up and she hissed at the pain that shot through her arm. It was a lot worse than she'd thought and far worse than she'd told Merrick.

A light knock on the door was followed by Merrick speaking. "I wish to see the wound."

"It's fine." She pressed the wad of tissues against

it. How long would she need to keep pressure on it to stop the bleeding? Or did it need stitches? She staggered to the toilet and sat on the closed lid, feeling sick at the sight of how much blood was seeping through the tissues.

"Audrey. Open the door," Merrick ordered.

"I'm fine." She lowered her head, feeling dizzy.

"Open the door or I will use my magic to open it."

Standing up, she threw the wad of tissues in the toilet before grabbing another lot and pressing them against her arm. Trying not to think about how much blood had been on the tissues, she opened the door. "I'm fine."

He pried her hand away from her arm. "You're not fine."

She stepped back from him. "You are not using magic." She had no idea what else to do. Medical help was out of the question. There was no way she could explain where they'd been during the past week or where their parents were.

"I can heal it." Siani peered around Merrick.

"You might make it worse," Merrick said.

"Who do you think healed me when I escaped from Gower's people?" Siani tried to push past him.

Merrick prevented Siani from entering the bathroom. "Luw."

"I might as well have waited until I was home and had someone skilled at healing do it if I'd waited until Luw found me," Siani said.

Merrick faced his niece. "Didn't Luw rescue you?"

"No. I ran when my mother told me to. Several of them chased after me, but I was too quick." Siani made a face. "They weren't willing to follow me through thorny shrubs that spread out over a large area. They tried to go around them."

"Why did Luw tell everyone he rescued you?" Audrey sat back on the closed lid of the toilet, her legs feeling weak and her head light. She'd gone back to keeping pressure on the wound.

Merrick entered the bathroom to crouch in front of her, taking her hand. "I never actually heard him say he did. Only everyone else." He stared at her for a moment. "You don't look fine even though you keep telling me you are."

Siani joined them, tugging Audrey's hand away from the wound. "I can fix that. It's easy enough." She placed her hand over the wound and the bathroom filled with the spicy, sweet scent of carnations.

"What are you-" Audrey broke off on a sharp, indrawn breath as her skin felt like it was being pulled and dragged back together. "Is it meant to feel like that?"

Jordan peered through the doorway. "Are you okay, Aude?"

She forced her lips into a smile. "Of course I am." Her jaw tightened and she tried not to make a sound.

Merrick leaned forward, his breath brushing across her cheek. "Siani isn't as good as someone skilled in healing. You would barely notice what they were doing."

She was lost for words. Didn't dare turn her head with how close he was. Although she was tempted. More than tempted.

Siani stepped back. "There. Healed."

Audrey gingerly touched her arm, pushing Merrick away from her so she could look at where the wound had been. There wasn't even a mark. "It's gone. Completely gone."

Siani grinned. "Of course it is. I told you I could heal it."

"Thank you." She met the Fae's gaze. "I didn't doubt you, I just didn't know what healing meant exactly."

"Making things as they once were," Siani said.

Audrey rose to her feet. "Thank you." She glanced at the vanity. "I need to get cleaned up."

Chapter Twenty-Two

Audrey waited until the bathroom was empty then closed the door and cleaned the blood off her hands and arm. She winced when the blood on the shirt stained her arm again. Sighing, she opened the door, planning to get a fresh shirt.

Jordan stood in front of the door, a hand raised as if about to knock, a shirt in the other hand. "I thought you might want something clean to put on."

"Thanks." She took the shirt from her brother. "Are you okay? Has everything been fine here?"

Jordan nodded. "Most of the time it's too strange to think about. The rest of the time I don't know what to think." His lips twisted into a fleeting smile. "There's no way I could ever tell any of this to Mike. He'd be an idiot about it."

Audrey grinned at him. "Mike is an idiot about everything."

"No, he isn't," Jordan argued.

Audrey's grin didn't fade. "Yes. He is." She glanced at the shirt she held. "I better finish getting cleaned up." She didn't want to risk Merrick doing magic.

Jordan nodded. He took a step away, glancing at the floor several times.

"What's wrong, Jordan?" She recognised his actions. There was something bothering him.

"You never actually said how Mum and Dad are." He stared at the floor. "And I never asked." He glanced up at her. "Does that make me a terrible person that I couldn't make myself ask?"

She rested a hand on his shoulder. "No. It makes you human." She tried not to think about what he was now he'd eaten Fae food. Did that make him something other than human? She shied away from the thought.

"Are they okay?" Jordan's question was barely loud enough to be heard.

"They will be." She glanced at her arm. "If the Fae can heal this well, they'll probably both be fine by the time I return to the castle."

"I should go with you," Jordan said.

"No, you should stay here and make sure Siani is safe. Her family are helping ours so it's the least we can do."

"I suppose."

"Of course it is. I bet they're clueless as to how things work in our world. They'd end up having the police carting them away or something."

Jordan chuckled. "Probably." He gestured to the shirt. "I'll leave you to finish cleaning up."

Nodding, she watched him stride along the hallway, closing the door before he was out of sight. At least one of them was less worried. Stripping off the shirt, she dropped it into the bathtub to rinse out later, cleaning the blood off her arm before pulling the shirt on. She didn't want to leave Merrick alone any longer than necessary. He hadn't seemed convinced of the seriousness of his problem.

Returning to her room, Audrey found Merrick standing by the edge of her curtain, staring out into the night through a gap. She paused in the doorway, not sure what to say.

Merrick turned to face her, his gaze resting on her arm. "There's no pain?"

She shook her head.

"I promised to never deliberately hurt you." A wry smile formed. "I suppose I should be grateful I never bound that promise with magic."

"I'm okay." She came far enough into the room that she could close the door. "Do you have a way of calling someone else here to take us back to the castle?"

"I can use my magic to return us to the castle and wait until then to stop using it."

She strode to her desk and took out the journal pages, flicking through them until she found the relevant pages. "Read this over then tell me it doesn't matter." She held the pages out to him.

He met her gaze as he took them from her. "It would be easiest if I took us back."

"Read the pages." She stepped away from him, glancing around for somewhere to sit while she waited for him to read the information. If it didn't convince him of the danger, she doubted anything would.

Merrick pulled out the chair that was tucked in under the desk, sitting down to read over the pages.

While she waited, she checked the messages on her phone. She turned it off. She had no idea how to answer the many questions and demands from her friends and family. Leaving the phone on the bedside cabinet, she looked over at Merrick who placed the pages on the desk near him.

"We don't know if this is the truth." He gestured towards the pages. "It's easy to lie through the written word."

"I doubt it's a lie." She glanced at the journal pages. "There's no way she would have expected anyone to steal the information. Not with how she kept it hidden. She didn't want anyone to read it let alone take it from her."

"Siani has trouble travelling to places through the use of magic and I doubt her knight would leave her here long enough to take us to the castle." He rose to his feet. "I might have to use my magic one last time."

She crossed the room, shaking her head. "No. You haven't seen the look in your eyes when you do magic."

"I can travel to a location where there'd be knights to restrain me so I don't harm you again," Merrick said.

"That isn't what I'm worried about." She looked up at him, meeting his gaze. "I don't want you to die."

He stared at her for a moment, not speaking. Eventually, he smiled. "You care."

She was unable to continue meeting his gaze, lowering hers to stare at the floor.

"Audrey, I am-"

She interrupted him, not wanting him to think she was expecting anything more than friendship. "I wouldn't want any of you to die. Not you, not your sister and not your niece."

"Audrey."

When he said nothing else, she looked up at him. Their gazes collided and she drew in a shuddering breath at the intense look in his eyes. She opened her mouth to speak, but not a single word formed.

He said her name again, closing the distance between them, his hand cupping her face. Again he spoke her name, the word soft as he lowered his head.

She leaned towards him, her lips meeting his and her arms automatically going around him. She felt his other arm encircle her waist, drawing her up against him. She clung to him, returning his kiss, thoughts of all their problems vanishing.

He continued to hold her tightly, drawing back his head to look down at her. "Will you remain in my realm once all this is over?"

"I don't know. Your realm isn't all that safe."

A grin fleetingly appeared and Merrick chuckled. "I don't think your realm is much safer."

"I understand my world. Yours doesn't make sense."

"No realm or world makes complete sense. Even to those making the rules." His grip on her tightened. "I would protect you. To my last breath."

"No. I'd never want that. Do you think I'd want anything to happen to you?"

He didn't answer immediately. "No, I don't suppose you would." His lips curved into a smile. "I could train you as a knight and we could protect each other."

"I like that idea much better."

He laughed softly. "I thought you might." His expression became serious. "I'll ask Siani if Tanwen gave her a way to communicate with her. I'd be surprised if she didn't."

"Like your leaf?"

"Yes."

When he continued to hold onto her, she smiled up at him. "You might have to let me go if you plan to talk to her."

He held her a moment longer before slowly letting go. Reaching the door, he turned back to face her. "Next time I'm not myself, don't put yourself in the way of my sword."

"Then don't threaten my brother and I won't have to."

He looked like he was about to argue. Instead, he inclined his head and left the room, closing the door behind him.

Alone, she collapsed on her bed, trying to figure out what she was thinking. She shouldn't have kissed him. Yet how could she have resisted? He was Fae.

From a completely different world. One that was more intriguing than her own, but also far more dangerous. She draped her arm over her eyes, trying to slow down her thoughts. It didn't help. Her mind was a swirl of contradictory thoughts. A knock on her bedroom door brought her to her feet. "Yes?"

"I accidentally sent the leaf to my mother when I was complaining about the knight always-" Siani broke off when Audrey opened the door.

"You have no way of contacting her?"

"She told me to return home if I was in danger. Other than that, she'll come visit me in a day or two, her time. Which means I have no real idea of when she'll be here," Siani said. "She can contact me, I just can't contact her. I need to stop calling her by her name when I become extremely annoyed with her."

"We're stuck here?" Audrey asked.

"No. My mother gave me directions to several natural portals to the realms of the Fae. I gave the directions to Merrick."

"They'll take us to the castle?"

Siani shook her head. "They'll take you to different locations in the realms of the Fae."

"We'll be able to get to the castle from one of them?"

"Yes. But it might be easier to wait for my mother to arrive," Siani suggested.

"You don't know how long it will be until she gets here." She needed to know how her parents were. And she needed to know soon, not days from now.

"Jordan would like you to stay. He's worried about you."

Audrey smiled, a wry one that disappeared before it had fully formed. "I know." She was worried about him too. "I won't be gone long. Then I'll come home."

Siani held out her hand, dark, glittery sand forming on her palm. "Did you want some of my magic since Merrick can't use his?"

She stared at the fine grains, not knowing what she should do. "Can you get rid of it if you decide you no longer want it?"

Siani shook her head. "Once you have magic, you always have magic. It becomes stronger over time, not weaker."

"I can do this without magic." It would make it impossible for her to live in her world if she had magic. If whatever Merrick had was similar to iron sickness, she'd be crazy if she accepted Siani's offer. Yet she couldn't help thinking how easy magic made travelling between places.

The dark, glittery grains sank back into Siani's hand. "Don't let him use his magic."

"I won't."

Siani stared at her silently for a moment, smiled, then left.

Chapter Twenty-Three

Audrey stared after the Fae. She had no idea what Siani had seen, but she'd obviously been happy with it. She sighed. At least someone was happy about something. She still had too many things she was worried about.

She headed to the lounge room, stopping in the doorway to stare at the images of her and her family on television.

Jordan looked up from the armchair. "We're on every channel. We won't be able to go anywhere without someone recognising us. Or our car. I'm surprised no one spotted you driving home."

Audrey momentarily closed her eyes. Yet one more thing to deal with. Maybe they'd be lucky and wouldn't have to go far to find a portal to the realms of the Fae. She turned to Merrick who sat in the lounge suite next to Siani. "How far away is the nearest portal to your world?"

Merrick nodded towards Jordan. "Your brother helped me figure out the location with the app on his phone. It seems to be a handy device. That is if you have no way of using magic."

Jordan held out his phone. "About an hour's drive."

She took the phone from him and checked the map, almost groaning. "That's in the middle of nowhere." They'd need to use the car. She dreaded to think what would happen if she was pulled over by the police. Driving without a license would be the least of her problems. How could she explain what had happened to her and her family?

Jordan took the phone back. "I've mapped out a route to take that should avoid cameras, tolls and speed traps. It will involve a lot of back streets and will take more than the usual hour."

"You could leave late at night, I've noticed your streets aren't as busy in the middle of the night," Siani said.

Jordan checked his phone. "If you leave at midnight, that will give you time for a sleep before you go. I can pack food for you to take with you."

She looked at each of the occupants in the room, including the Fae knight who stood in the corner, surveying the area. He obviously took his duties as a bodyguard very seriously. She turned to Merrick. "This will work?" She gestured towards the phone Jordan continued to hold. "Going through one of these portals."

Merrick nodded, rising to his feet and crossing the room to stand in front of her. "People use them all the time. Some of them are cursed and you need to be careful how you use them. The one we're going to isn't. Tanwen only gave Siani a list of safe portals."

It didn't take long to come to a decision. It wasn't like she had many options to choose between. "Okay. We'll leave here a little after midnight." She took a step back from Merrick. "I'll have a sleep before we go." She couldn't meet his gaze, feeling awkward after their earlier kiss. Glancing up at him, she quickly looked away, fleeing to her room. Once inside, with the door closed, she sighed heavily. A firm knock on the door had her spinning to face it.

"Audrey?"

She was tempted to sigh again at hearing Merrick's voice. "Yes?"

"Can I enter?"

She nearly said no. She half opened the door, remaining in the doorway.

He glanced past her. "Can I come in?"

She nearly said no again. Not because she didn't want him to come in, but because she wanted him to come in too much. The two of them would eventually go their own way. She was certain of it. And when that happened, she'd probably be devastated. Stepping back, she held the door wide open, waiting until he was in before she closed it.

"Is something wrong?"

She alternated between wanting to deliberately misunderstand him and telling him how she felt. She did neither, remaining silent instead.

"Audrey." He reached for her, lowering his hand before he made contact. "Have I done something wrong?"

Guilt swamped her. She knew exactly how he felt. The uncertainty. "Sorry. I just-" She broke off, making a vague gesture with her hand as she tried to think of how to explain her feelings. "When this is over, we'll probably never see each other again. We live in two completely different worlds."

"Do you want to see me after this is done?"

She had no idea, but guessed she should say something rather than leave him wondering. "I might not want to have anything to do with your world once my family are safe."

"I asked about me, not my realm."

She reached for him, capturing his hand when he reached for her too, his hand overly warm compared to how cold hers was. "I don't know." She tried to figure out what his expression meant, but she often struggled to understand what humans were thinking half the time so she probably had no way of knowing what a Fae thought. "All I can focus on right now is saving my family. I need to get back to the castle and figure out how to cure my dad." If she was lucky, all that was wrong with her mum was that she needed food and rest.

His gaze roamed her face, his lips curving slightly into a smile. "Then I guess we save your family so I can ask this question again."

Her breath caught at the look he gave her and she had no problem trying to figure out the meaning. He was very interested and wanted her to answer yes. She was tempted to give him the answer he wanted, but she looked away from him instead. There were other things to focus on. "You should have a sleep too."

"I can't."

She examined his face, seeing the fatigue. She frowned. "You're not tired?"

"I'm tired. I just can't sleep."

"Why not?" He remained silent long enough she started to ask him again.

"I might use my magic. It's a burning need, like I have to use it or it will eat away at me. An itch that's impossible to scratch."

She caught a glimpse of the wildness in the depths of his eyes. Her grip tightened on his hand. She'd thought his was warm because hers were cold. But her hand had warmed up now and his was still warmer than hers. "You can't use it."

"What if I use a little, just to reduce the sensation so I can sleep? I could create a leaf for you to replace the one you sent back to me. The one I used to bring me to you."

"No." She stepped closer, resting her other hand against his chest. "Promise me you won't use any magic."

A smile briefly appeared. "Most Fae promises are bound by magic."

"I don't need you to bind your promise or whatever it is you'd normally do. I want you to stop using magic until whatever Madlen did to you is over." Her hand against his chest tightened into a fist, bunching the material of his shirt. "Promise me. Without magic."

He untangled her hand from his shirt, bringing it to his lips. He held her gaze as he touched his lips to her hand, raising his head slightly. "I promise."

A shiver ran through her at the look he gave her and she tried to speak. Words failed, her mind emptying of thoughts when his lips curved into a smile. She tried to tell herself that she shouldn't, that she should wait until all this was over before she decided anything. But she found herself leaning towards him, her lips meeting his as he also leaned in. Eventually, she drew away. "I need to sleep. You should too."

He ran his fingers along the side of her face and with another smile, left.

She stared at the closed door, fighting the urge to call him back. She needed sleep. Who knew how long it'd be before she'd have the chance for another one. There was a lot needing to be done. Look how long it had taken to reach the castle last time they hadn't been able to use magic.

Sleep came quicker than she expected and she was woken by a knock on her door. Stumbling to her feet, she rubbed at her eyes as she crossed the room. A glance at her alarm clock showed it was almost midnight. Uneasiness curled through her. She wasn't up to this. Who did she think she was that she could return to the realms of the Fae and find a way to cure whatever Madlen had done to her dad?

Another knock sounded on the door. "You awake, Aude?"

She opened the door to find her brother in the hallway looking like he was in need of sleep. "You look terrible."

He grinned at her. "You don't look any better." The humour in his expression faded. "Did you want me to come with you? I can pack another backpack with food. Not that I'd have any trouble finding food to eat now."

"You need to stay here with Siani."

"You're only saying that to keep me out of danger." A wry smile briefly appeared. "I'm not a little kid. You don't have to protect me. I can protect you too you know."

She rested her hand on his shoulder. "I know. You've rescued me on more than one occasion." She lightly squeezed his shoulder. "We don't belong there. Look what's happened to us there."

"Part of it happened here," Jordan said.

"Yes, but it was from one of the Fae."

"Not all of them are bad."

She couldn't help thinking of Merrick. "I know."

"I'll let you finish getting ready. There's a backpack in the kitchen for you. A sandwich too. And I also charged the car battery. It should last long enough to get you to the portal."

"Okay." She turned to watch him return along the hallway, catching sight of Merrick at the end of it. She wanted to ask him how long he'd been there.

He remained where he was until Jordan was out of sight then strode towards her. "Is that your answer?"

"Logically, it should be."

"Are you always logical?"

Laughter escaped as a few incidents came to mind. "I'm afraid not."

"Then I'll have to hope this is one of those instances where you choose to be illogical."

Her gaze roamed his face. "Have you slept?"

"No."

She started to tell him he could sleep in the car. Taking a deep breath, she glanced away. "I'll meet you in the kitchen."

Inclining his head, he strode in the direction Jordan had taken.

She remained in the doorway a moment longer before she readied herself for the coming journey. Reaching the kitchen, she discovered a printed map, which had a route highlighted, on the table beside a bulging cloth backpack. She gathered both items. On the end of the table was a plate with a sandwich.

Merrick took the backpack from her, slinging it over a shoulder. "Do you need to do anything else before we leave?"

She picked up the sandwich, taking a bite before she took a small torch from a drawer in the kitchen and collected the keys that were hanging in their usual place on a hook in one of the glass fronted cupboards. She assumed her brother had returned them since she'd left them in the ignition. "No. I have everything." She glanced around the room, disappointed her brother wasn't here to see her off. She led the way to the garage, finishing her food before she reached it.

Jordan leaned against the car. "Are you sure you don't need me to come with you." He straightened.

"Positive." She stopped in front of Jordan, glad to see him. "Don't let anyone know you're back until Mum and Dad are home."

"What are we going to tell everyone?"

She shrugged. "We'll worry about that when we're back." She hugged her brother, something he let her do only rarely. She tried not to think of how scared he must be to have let her hug him. "I'll see you soon."

He nodded, striding to the garage door and opening it.

Chapter Twenty-Four

Getting in the front seat, Audrey tried to ignore the uneasiness that remained with her. She glanced at Merrick when he sat in the passenger seat, holding the map out to him. "Can you direct?" She held the torch out when he took the map.

"I won't need that."

"Why? Can you see in the dark?" Her question was half teasing.

"Well enough."

"Oh." Not knowing what to think, let alone say, she started the engine and drove out.

Other than Merrick's directions, the drive was silent, taking them an hour and three quarters. They turned off a narrow, single lane road onto a dirt track, parking under a cluster of trees at the end of it.

Turning off the engine, Audrey sat in the darkness. Outside she heard the sound of rushing water and the noises of night animals. A curlew cried out nearby, sending a chill down her spine.

"Are you ready?" Merrick asked.

She nodded, worried that she'd say 'no' if she tried to speak. Picking up the torch, she'd dropped onto her lap earlier, she got out of the car, locking it and returning the key to its hiding place. Who knew where they'd end up and if they'd need to travel back to this location.

Merrick led the way down a narrow track to the river, the backpack in place and his steps sure.

Audrey followed, glaring at his back when she slipped on the loose stones. How did he make it look so easy? The light from her torch bobbed across the ground that was rutted and uneven, sections washed away. Yet the goat track didn't seem to hamper him in the least.

Merrick paused by the river, watching her stumble down the last couple of metres. "The portal will lead us to the Fringes. You need to avoid making eye contact with anyone and definitely don't stare at them." His hand rested on the hilt of his sword.

"Why?"

"Some of those who live in the Fringes are a little crazy. Many of them are suffering from iron sickness."

She thought of the Demi Fae who'd escaped Madlen. "That's a bit of an understatement," she muttered.

Merrick chuckled, holding out a hand to her. "Ready?"

"No." She placed her hand in his. "So let's get this over and done with."

It didn't take long to find the cave. The opening was large and the ground sandy. They strode to the back, avoiding the remains of old fires and broken beer bottles.

Merrick let go of her hand to run his over the tumble of boulders at the back of the cave, most of them towering over him. "Here. This gap is large enough for us to squeeze through." He removed the backpack, holding it by the straps.

"No one said we had to go through a tunnel." Audrey backed away.

Merrick faced her. "You can remain here and I'll return to the castle and your parents. I can walk you back to your car first if you'd like."

She froze, her gaze on the boulders behind him. She wanted to tell him she was going with him, but the words wouldn't form. Tears did instead.

"Audrey?"

She squeezed her eyes closed at the way he said her

name. "I can't." Her hand curled into a fist, the other tightening on the torch as she opened her eyes. "I need to, but I can't."

"It isn't long. Several feet."

"What is that in metres?"

He shrugged.

She sighed heavily. Maybe that was better, not knowing the exact distance. She took a step towards him, turning off the torch. "Help me, please?" The darkness closed in on her and she tried to convince herself that she was in the middle of the cave. Plenty of space around her.

Merrick took hold of her hand. "You don't have to do this. You can return home and I'll see that your parents are brought to you."

"What about Dad? What if he's still the same?"

"I'll figure something out."

She wanted to tell him to take her back to the car. Every part of her wanted to run. Was poised to flee. "Take me to your world." She felt him move close.

"Gladly."

She shivered at the tone he used, a smile almost forming. Fear crashed in on her again as he tugged her forward. It took all her self-control not to wrench her hand from his grip.

He tightened his hold on her. "Is there anything

you like about the realms of the Fae?" He guided her forward.

"Can't we have this conversation later?"

"What if I was to take you to my home? Maybe you'd like it better."

His words startled her and she stumbled forward several steps. "You have your own home?"

"It isn't as large as my parents' castle. Could be considered a cottage in comparison."

The boulders pressed against her. "I can't do-" She broke off. "In comparison? How big is it? Are you lying about it being a cottage?"

"Have you forgotten I can't lie?"

"No. But you pretty much said there were ways around it." Her breath came too fast and her heart raced, but somehow she continued to inch through the tunnel, trying to focus on his words.

"How about I show you one day instead of describing it?"

"Is that your way of getting me to return?"

"Would you return without an incentive?"

She tried to say 'no', but the word wouldn't form. And not because of how she struggled to keep moving through the tunnel. "Why do you have your own house?"

"I didn't say house. I said home. It was a gift from

my parents when I turned eighteen so I'm still making it mine. It's within riding distance of the knight I've been training with for the past few years."

"I'll be lucky if my parents buy me a car for my eighteenth." She opened her eyes when Merrick placed her hand on the edge of a rock. A glimmer of light showed through a gap.

"I need to let go of you while I exit the tunnel. Hold onto the wall and don't let go."

"We're nearly out?" The glimmer of light was blocked and she realised it was from Merrick squeezing through the exit. "I can't–"

Merrick took hold of her hand, prying it from the edge of the wall. "Climb through."

It was worse when there was enough light to see how cramped her surroundings were. She closed her eyes, trying not to think of how everything pressed in on her.

"Audrey. Climb through. Come on. You're nearly out."

She focused on his voice, stumbling through the opening. Bursting free, she tugged her hand from his, grinning at having made it through the tunnel. "I can't believe–" She broke off when someone ran into her.

He grabbed hold of her, having come around a nearby corner at a run. "Watch it," he growled.

She stared open-mouthed at the figure that held her. He had wings that were folded at his back to drape across him like a feathered cloak, a narrow hawk like face and feathery hair. He might have had a human shaped body, but he made her think of a bird of prey.

He looked her up and down, a grin forming. "Pretty little pet, who do you belong to?"

Merrick drew his sword. "Unhand her, Raptor. She has my protection."

The Raptor continued to hold onto her. "Only has your protection? Then who owns her?"

She wanted to argue that no one owned her, but she had no idea how things worked around here. "Audrey owns me."

Merrick chuckled. "You heard the human. You'd best unhand her."

"I've never heard of an Audrey. Who is she?"

"Someone you don't want to mess with. It could have fatal consequences for you." Merrick met her gaze momentarily before returning his attention to the Raptor. "So I suggest you unhand the human immediately."

The Raptor shoved Audrey towards Merrick before striding away.

Audrey waited until he was out of sight before she turned to Merrick. "I thought you couldn't lie."

"I can't."

"Then how would messing with me have fatal consequences for him?"

"If he harmed you I would make him feel every hurt ten times over."

She opened her mouth several times before she could form a coherent reply. "You would kill him?"

"Only if it was necessary."

"But…" Again words failed her.

"Would you prefer I let him kill you instead?"

"Of course not. But surely there are other options. What about the law?"

He sheathed his sword. "This isn't your human realm with its many rules that you all tend to break as often as you pay attention to them. The closest we have to a law is the wild hunt and you never want to have them coming after you."

She didn't know if she wanted to know who, or what, the wild hunt was.

He glanced around the area. "We're not far from Idris. We should visit him while we're so close."

"Why?"

"We owe him for leading us to your father."

She tried to convince herself that Merrick was right, but all she wanted to do was argue his comment. How long had it been since she'd seen her parents? Especially with how time worked between her world and his.

"Audrey?" He waited until she met his gaze before he continued to speak. "Shall we call on him?"

"I suppose."

He picked up the backpack that rested on the cobblestone street next to a crack in a stone and mortar wall. "This way. And remember not to look at anyone too long."

She moved closer to him. "I don't plan to look at them at all."

He laughed softly. "Maybe look at them long enough that you don't risk running into them."

"That wasn't my fault. He ran-" She broke off as they stepped into a crowded area, a mix of races milling around. "Where are we?"

"Courtyard markets. You can buy nearly anything here."

Chapter Twenty-Five

Stalls were scattered around the outside of the area displaying all types of wares and shops were open in the buildings that edged the open area, inexpertly painted signs hanging above their doors. The markets were filled with people, their voices creating a blur of noise, flickering campfires at various points around the area even with the early morning light banishing many of the shadows.

Remembering Merrick's advice, Audrey lowered her gaze rather than stare at the people milling about the stalls and shops, entertainers mingling with them. "Is this where you shop?"

Merrick slid an arm around her waist, having slipped the backpack into place. "This is where most sane Fae and Demi Fae tend to avoid. There are numerous towns throughout the realms where things can be purchased. Less dangerous places."

She remained at his side as they crossed the markets, trying not to comment when they were stopped twice by Fae interested in purchasing her. She pressed her lips together on the words that wanted to spill.

They stepped into a narrow alley and Merrick glanced down at her. "Are you all right?"

"Have you sold a human before?" she demanded.

"My family don't believe in keeping humans as pets, but we have bought humans who were in situations they needed to escape."

She pulled away from him. "You own humans?"

"They are our protégés and were given the option of leaving or staying. We pay them for the work they do around the castle."

"Oh."

He captured her hand, holding it lightly. "Things are different to your world. There is both good and bad. But what might be bad in your world might actually be considered good in this world."

"How can slavery be good?"

"My parents bought a violinist from another Fae decades ago. He was given the option of returning to his world or remaining with them and entertaining them with his music. He chose to remain where he could spend his days composing and playing his music. He's their protégé. They would protect him from other Fae that might try and steal him for their own entertainment."

"What about those who don't have a talent?" She couldn't stop thinking of his offer for her to be his protégé.

"Everyone has a talent. Some need the time and space to discover what their talent is." He nodded in the direction they'd been heading. "We haven't far to go."

She fell in beside him, scanning the area they walked through. Some of the cobblestone streets weren't much wider than the few alleys they hurried along. The buildings towered above them, some in need of repair, others gutted by fire. She was almost relieved to reach Idris' place, that relief vanishing when he opened the door and she saw the wild look in his eyes.

He reached for his dagger. "You think to come after me again?"

"We came to repay you for your help," Merrick said.

The Demi Fae left his hand on the hilt of his dagger he'd started to draw. "Repay?"

Merrick inclined his head. "Your information led

us to the person we needed to find so we've come to repay your help."

He let the dagger slide back into the sheath. "How do you think you can repay me?"

"I read Madlen's journal," Audrey said.

"Did she talk of me?" Idris came close, peering into her face. "Are you one of hers? Is this another trap?"

She wanted to growl in frustration. How did Merrick think they could tell Idris anything when he didn't trust them? "She didn't name anyone. Just called them experiments."

Idris nodded. "Yes. We are only what she can learn from us. Nothing unless we can provide more knowledge for her studies. Did she study you?"

She wanted to look away from the wild look in his eyes. It reminded her too much of their previous encounter. "No. I escaped before she could." Not that she was certain Madlen would have experimented on her even if she hadn't been interested in selling her. Some of the humans had been kept for comparison to those she'd experimented on. Her control subjects.

"I was one of her experiments," Merrick said.

"You're hers?" Idris demanded. "She sent you?"

Audrey was tempted to grab him by the shoulders and shake him. "It's the magic. That's the key. You can't use your magic until whatever she's done to you is cured. It could take weeks. Less if you're lucky."

Idris grabbed her chin and held her face in his grip as he peered into her eyes. "You might speak the truth."

"Let her go," Merrick demanded.

She waved Merrick back when she heard the threatening tone of his voice. The last thing she wanted was a repeat of the previous encounter. "Don't use your magic and you'll be cured. Keep using it and what she did to you will kill you."

His grip tightened painfully on her chin. "You don't have the look of one of hers."

"I'm not hers. Thanks to you I was able to rescue someone from her."

"Does she know? Did it anger her?"

"Yeah, she knows. But I think taking her journal angered her more than taking the captives from her."

Idris chuckled. "Good. She needs to know what it's like." He let go of her chin, but didn't step back. "It burns, you know. The magic. When you don't use it. I have the magic collector take it from me. He pays me for it."

"He can use it?" Merrick asked.

Idris shrugged, returning his attention to Audrey. "She's mad?"

"Yes." She was tempted to say she was mad in both senses of the word.

"She's mad." Idris grinned, repeating the words as he turned away, closing the door on them.

Audrey remained where she was, staring at the closed door. "That's it?"

"We've repaid our debt."

"It doesn't feel like it." She turned her back on the door. "He doesn't seem any better off than he was before." She looked in both directions. "How far is the castle from here?"

"It'd take us a couple of days to walk that far." He looked along the road. "I could see if the magic collector is willing to buy some of my magic. Even with whatever Madlen has done it must still be usable if he's accepting Idris' magic."

"People buy magic?" She stared at him, shaking her head when the concept still didn't make sense. "Why?"

"Because they don't have any or they want more." Merrick headed along the cobblestone street, staying in the middle, continually scanning the area. Some of the buildings lining the street looked like they might collapse.

"What are you looking for?" She checked the area

too, seeing no one. It was much quieter around here than the courtyard markets.

"Anyone who might attack us."

The Raptor who'd grabbed her earlier came to mind, making her pick up her pace. "How much further do we need to go until we reach the magic collector?"

"Not far."

She remained silent, continually checking over her shoulder and half expecting to be attacked. They reached a dilapidated house that had a lantern hanging by the front door, a candle burning in it even though it was day.

Merrick knocked on the door, knocking a second time when no one answered.

"Maybe the magic collector isn't home."

"He is. The lantern is lit. That means he's home." Merrick knocked again.

The door jerked open. "What do you want?" A middle-aged man with scraggly, reddish-brown hair and a matching beard, grey sprinkled through it, glared at them. His beard and hair were badly trimmed and he wore an old-fashioned suit coat that was frayed at the edges. "Well?"

"You've been buying magic from Idris," Merrick said.

"What of it?"

"My magic is the same as his."

"What do you want me to do about it?" the magic collector demanded.

"We need a way to get to Carralin Castle. We have no money and no transport," Merrick said.

"Are you offering to sell me some of your magic?" the magic collector asked.

Merrick nodded. "Is it usable?"

"After it has sat for a turn of the moon. I can't use it immediately so I can't give you full price for it." The magic collector opened the door wide. "Come in if you're interested."

Audrey followed Merrick inside the house, her gaze drawn around the room. There were animals in cages and a table in the middle of the room. Even though she wanted to ask what the caged animals were for, she kept quiet, preferring not to draw the magic collector's attention. There was something about him she didn't like.

"Call out your magic." The magic collector placed a small glass bottle on the table. "And put it in that."

Merrick shook his head. "I can't use it. Not with what was done to it."

The magic collector drew three small glass bottles from a pocket of his suit coat along with a white crystal and placed them on the table too. "Someone else will have to use the crystal." He looked pointedly at Audrey. "I don't want any magic. Not in this area."

"How do you use it?" The crystal reminded her of an ordinary quartz crystal from her world.

The magic collector picked up one of the bottles and the crystal, holding both in one hand, the crystal pressed to the outside of the bottle. "Place the crystal against his skin and it will draw the magic from him and store it in the bottle." He returned the two objects to the table.

When Audrey started to pick them up, Merrick grabbed her hand. She met his gaze. "What's wrong?"

"I can do it myself." Merrick let go of her.

The magic collector shook his head. "Idris tried. It doesn't work like that. The magic fights you."

She picked up the crystal and one of the bottles. "I can do this. How hard can it be?"

Merrick drew her to the side of the room, glancing at the magic collector before he spoke, keeping his voice low. "You'll risk ending up with magic if you're not careful. My damaged magic. And who knows what it might do to you with how damaged it currently is."

"How do I avoid that?"

"By not letting your fingers touch me, only the

crystal. And draw it away from me when the magic nears the top of the bottle. You don't want it to overflow."

"Are you collecting the magic or not?" the magic collector demanded. "I have other things to do."

"I'll take us to my parents' estate with my magic. One more time won't hurt," Merrick said.

Chapter Twenty-Six

Audrey met Merrick's gaze. "No. You can't." She wasn't about to let him risk using his magic. Holding the bottle and crystal the same way the magic collector had held them, she grabbed Merrick's arm and pushed his sleeve back before pressing the crystal against his wrist. The magic flowed into the bottle, rapidly filling it. Before she could draw the crystal away, it was overflowing onto her hand.

"Don't waste it." The magic collector snatched one of the bottles off the table and held it out to her.

Pins and needles pricked along her hand where the magic had touched her and sank into her skin. She tried not to think about what that meant. Exchanging bottles with the magic collector, she filled another. Once again it rapidly filled, overflowing before she could draw it away. "Is it meant to fill so fast?"

"No." Both Merrick and the magic collector answered at the same time.

"Am I doing something wrong?" She pressed the crystal and the third bottle against Merrick's wrist.

"It wants to be used." The magic collector put lids on each of the bottles. "It thinks you're going to use it since he won't."

Finished filling the bottles, Audrey returned the crystal. She tried to ask if she now had magic, but couldn't bring herself to voice the question. What if they said yes? What would she do? What could she do? From everything she'd been told, magic was forever.

The magic collector scribbled on a piece of paper he took from a drawer in a bench along the side of the room. "Give this to whoever is greeting customers at Masquerade. They'll see that you get a lift on a wagon going near Carralin Castle. To the nearby town."

Merrick took the piece of paper. "Thank you."

Audrey waited until they were outside and well away from the house before she spoke. "What is Masquerade?"

"A nightclub. It's a sanctuary."

"A sanctuary for what?"

"Everyone. No one can harm another there. It's where the hunted go to remain safe."

"There's a safe place in the realms of the Fae?"

Merrick chuckled. "It's a rare place indeed. In this realm or yours."

A smile reluctantly formed. "My world isn't that bad."

He gave her a look of disbelief. "I've read about your many wars and listened to Fae who fought in some of them. One of my parents' knights fought in your first world war. He said these new wars aren't like the ones of old. Such as the ones he fought in during your middle ages."

She stared at him, mouth open as she tried to comprehend how old the knight must be. "He's still alive?"

"No one has managed to kill him off yet. He doesn't stay in your world long these days, the iron sickness tends to hit him quicker than it once did."

His words reminded her of the magic she'd taken from him and she finally found the courage to ask her earlier question. "Do I have magic?" She began to think he wasn't going to answer. She glanced at him several times as they continued along the middle of the cobblestone road.

"I'm sorry. I didn't know it would be like that. Normally magic trickles out, not gushes."

"It wasn't your fault."

"I should have used my magic to take us to my parents' estate."

"No." The word burst from her and she grabbed his hand, linking her fingers through his. "Don't even think about it." She hesitated. "Does that mean I have to live here now?"

"You can keep your magic low and spend most of your time in your world. You will have to reduce the amount of iron in your environment and visit the realms of the Fae regularly."

"Oh."

"At least you'll be able to eat what you want now."

She stared at him, returning to watching where she was going when she stumbled on a loose cobblestone. "Are you sure?" She didn't feel any different.

"When we reach the castle you can see for yourself."

She didn't know if she wanted to risk it. Not in this world where magic was used for healing. Maybe it only worked on wounds. She remained silent rather than disagree. They could argue about it later.

She was about to ask him how much longer when they approached a building that was three storeys high, had two balconies across the front of both the upper floors and a rooftop garden. A timber sign hung above the door and 'Masquerade' was written on it in gold. "This is a nightclub?"

Merrick nodded.

"Will I be allowed in there? I'm not eighteen."

"What has that to do with anything?" He held the door open for her.

She stepped inside. "Everything. In my world."

He grinned at her. "You're in my realm now."

Before she could comment, a young man asked if they wanted a table. Audrey looked around the area while Merrick explained what they wanted. It seemed ordinary after the impression she'd gained from the exterior and she tried to peer through the doorway that was behind a counter. There was nothing to see.

Merrick shook hands with the young man behind the counter and ushered Audrey outside.

She glanced over her shoulder as the door was closed. "What's happening?" She should have paid attention instead of trying to find out where the doorway led.

"We need to hurry. The cart leaves shortly." Merrick strode along at a fast pace.

She had to nearly run to keep up with him, but they made it before the cart left, handing over the piece of paper from the magic collector. She clambered up onto the back of the cart, sitting amongst the crates of fruit and vegetables. When Merrick settled in beside her, she turned to him. "Wouldn't the town near your castle be able to get fruit and vegetables from somewhere closer?"

"These are ones suitable for humans. For those without magic."

"Oh."

The journey was monotonous and Audrey eventually fell asleep to the rumble of the cart as it travelled over uneven dirt roads, occasionally travelling over cobblestone ones. She woke when the cart stopped, surprised to find they were at the castle. She waited until the cart drove off before she spoke, keeping her voice low so as not to be heard by the knight who had come to greet them and hand coins to the driver before he left. "I thought he was taking us to the town."

"I convinced him to bring us here. That's why the knight paid him." Merrick slipped an arm around her waist. "Did you want to find out how your parents are or did you want a wash first?"

There was a fine layer of dust over her and even though she knew she should see her parents, she didn't know if she was up to finding out how they were doing. She was still coming to terms with having magic and didn't want to risk being told about any more problems. "A wash."

"I'll escort you to your room." Merrick paused inside the entrance of the castle, beckoning a servant over and requesting a bath be organised for Audrey.

"Thank you."

He held both her hands, facing her and meeting her gaze. "No. I'm the one who must thank you. Not only did you rescue me, but you searched for the reason behind my illness. Thank you." He lowered his head.

She tilted hers up, meeting his lips and returning his kiss. She untangled her hands from his to slide them around his waist, drawing him close.

"Audrey!"

At her mum's sharp cry, Audrey reluctantly drew away from Merrick, a grin momentarily appearing. She managed to force the grin away before she faced her mum, looking her up and down. "You're better?"

"Where have you been? That knight said you weren't in the basement when he returned to collect you."

Merrick stepped in front of Audrey. "Your daughter is extremely brave."

"You said you'd take care of her." Joan's eyes narrowed. "And did you?"

Audrey stepped around Merrick to stand at his side. "I can take care of myself. Obviously. I'm here, aren't I?" She didn't mention the magic she'd gained. Not that it counted. She had taken care of herself. She'd lived.

"Where is Jordan? No one will tell me anything and they have your father locked up like some criminal," Joan said.

"Jordan is at home and Dad would kill someone if they let him out." Audrey tried not to sigh. "I need a wash. I'm covered in dust from our ride."

"You've been out sightseeing while your father and I have been stuck here?" Joan demanded.

"Of course I haven't." Audrey glared at her mum. "I've been trying to get back to you. And to Dad."

"Then you shouldn't have left the basement. You should have been there when the knight returned."

"Luw," Audrey said.

"What are you talking about?" Joan asked.

"The knight. His name is Luw." Audrey glanced at Merrick when he took hold of her hand and lightly squeezed it, smiling at him in thanks.

Joan's gaze momentarily focused on their hands. "We need to leave. Immediately."

Audrey's grip tightened on Merrick's hand. She wasn't about to let anyone tell her who she could date. She would figure that out on her own. "Once Dad is better."

"You can't expect me to leave Jordan at home on his own." Joan once more glanced at Audrey's hand in Merrick's.

Audrey was pretty sure that wasn't the main reason. Not with how her mum kept looking at their hands. "He isn't on his own. There's a Fae knight with him." It was probably best not to mention there was also a Fae around his own age with him. A female Fae at that. She barely managed not to smile at the thought.

"As I said, I'm not about to leave him home on his own."

Any thoughts of smiling fled. "I'm having a wash." Keeping hold of Merrick's hand, she strode towards the doorway.

"I haven't finished talking to you, Audrey." Joan followed.

Merrick beckoned a knight forward. "Detain her."

Joan called after her, also demanding the knight let her go.

Audrey knew she should protest. "The knight won't hurt her, will he?"

"No." Merrick didn't speak again until they were at the door of the bedroom Audrey had used previously. "I'll let them know your father needs as much magic drained off as possible. And to avoid getting it on them."

"Will that help?"

"It helped me. I no longer feel like it's burning through me."

She winced at the thought. "Will that happen to me?"

He shrugged. "If it does, we'll deal with it. But maybe it'll be different for you. We know it shouldn't be used so if you don't use it, things might be easier."

"Thank you."

He took her hand, holding it between both of his. "I'm sorry you ended up with magic."

"I've already told you, it isn't your fault."

"If there was a way to take it from you, I would." He glanced past her at the open doorway. "You might want to have a wash while the water is warm."

She nodded, reluctantly letting go of him and watching him walk away. Once he was out of sight, she closed the door and stripped out of her dusty clothes, relieved to see there was another set laid out on the bed.

Chapter Twenty-Seven

It didn't take Audrey long to wash and she'd barely finished dressing in trousers and a shirt, slipping her sneakers back on, when someone knocked on the door. Expecting it to be her mum, she opened the door, ready to continue the argument.

Luw looked her over. "You left the basement."

"I hope I didn't get you in trouble."

He shrugged. "Your mother has been full of complaints."

Audrey grinned. That didn't surprise her. "Sorry."

"I was told Siani is with your brother. In a safe location."

"Yeah."

"Are you certain it's safe?"

"No one knows where it is."

"Except you," Luw said.

"I'm not the only one." Wanting to change the

subject, since she had no intention of telling him where Jordan and Siani were in case someone overheard, she asked, "Why did you tell everyone you rescued Siani?"

"I never told anyone that."

"But they all think you did."

Luw shrugged. "I'm not responsible for what people think." He slipped a hand into his pocket. "Would you make me responsible for their thoughts?"

"No. Of course not. It's just that I thought you'd tell them they were wrong whenever they mentioned it."

"Why would they mention it to me?" Luw asked.

She had no idea how to answer that question. Before she could come up with a reply, he spoke again.

"Can you show me where Siani is?"

"Why?"

"How do I know the knight who went with her has checked the area thoroughly and made it safe for her to remain there?" He withdrew his hand from his pocket, the scent of his magic filling the hallway. "All you need to do is picture where she is and I can take us both there."

"She's safe. The less people who know her

whereabouts, the better." She took a step back from him.

"Are you trying to tell me you can't picture the location?"

"I said exactly what I meant." She started to close the door.

Before it could close, Luw grabbed hold of her arm and the world shimmered around them, reforming as a dungeon. A flickering stub of a candle was placed in the middle of the floor and a woman was curled up asleep next to it. "Where is she?" Luw demanded, shaking Audrey hard.

She tried to pull out of his grip. He was too strong. "Let me go."

"Not until you take me to her."

"I'm not about to take you anywhere near her." She glanced at the woman who stirred, recognising her as the human who'd helped her free Tanwen from Gower. "You're the one who told Gower where they'd be and how many of them were going to be in the party."

"Are you willing to die to protect her location?" Luw demanded.

She pressed her lips tightly together. She might not be willing to die to protect Siani, but she wasn't about to put her brother's life in danger.

The woman struggled to her feet, reaching for Luw. "My lord, you've returned. Tell your father he can't hold me responsible for the girl stealing my key when the knights arrived. I wasn't looking in her direction when she took it."

He shook her off. "You should have been more vigilant." He continued to hold onto Audrey, his gaze never leaving her. "You had best answer my question. Where is Siani?"

She met his gaze, raising her chin. "I guess you'll have to kill me."

Luw's lips curved into a smile. "I think I'll organise something worse." He pushed her from him.

She staggered, but remained on her feet as he strode for the door. "If Gower is your father, why hasn't anyone mentioned it?"

He turned to glare at her. "He will acknowledge me once we have the castle. Then he'll name me his heir." With another glare at her, he faced the door and banged on it. "Open up." There was the sound of running footsteps followed by the door opening.

"My lord." The Fae bowed deeply. "What are you doing in here?"

Luw gestured towards Audrey. "See that iron bands are put on her. Then organise the torturer." He strode from the dungeon.

She stared after him, open-mouthed. They were going to torture her?

"You must care for Siani deeply," the woman said.

It took her a few attempts to speak. "I care for my brother who is with her." She tried to think clearly, but Luw's final words rang out in her mind, over and over. "I need to get out of here."

"Did Tanwen reach safety? Her and the baby?"

Audrey stared at the woman. "Baby?"

The woman nodded. "She's several months along." She nodded towards the door. "He doesn't know or he would have killed her rather than have planned to use her to create a trap for the child. I helped her hide the morning sickness."

Audrey wanted to sit on the floor and drop her head into her hands. Things were getting worse by the minute. "We have to get out of here."

"Unless you can escape through the drainage hole, there's no way out of here." The woman gestured towards the hole off to one side of the dungeon.

"It's too small. My hips would get stuck." The rest of her might get through though. She shuddered. If she could bring herself to go down there. "What's it used for?"

"It's a drain for when they throw buckets of water

in here to wash the blood away after the torturer has been."

The woman's words brought another shudder. "Can we use magic to escape?"

The woman held out her hands, iron bands around her wrists. "I can't use it while wearing these. My magic isn't strong enough to fight against the interference of the iron."

Footsteps had Audrey running to the door to peer through the bars of the small window. It was the same Fae as before. He carried two iron bands and a ring of keys. Crazy ideas ran through her mind. She pressed herself against the wall beside the door, listening as he used the keys to unlock it. The door swung inward and she looked from the keys left in the lock to the Fae that entered. He stopped just past the door, doing a slow turn.

Knowing it wouldn't be long before he spotted her, Audrey threw herself at the door, wrenching the keys from the lock and throwing them towards the woman. The Fae crashed into her, the two armbands clattering across the floor. She struggled to escape his grip, kicking at him as she tried to rise from the floor where they'd landed.

In the corridor was the sound of running footsteps. Audrey had no idea who was coming, but she didn't have time to wait around and see. She needed to get out of here before she faced too many Fae and had no chance to escape. Bursting free from his grip, she spun to face the doorway.

The woman grabbed her arm, tugging her away from the Fae who lunged towards her. "Trust me."

The air was filled with a summery smell that reminded Audrey of sunshine and growing plants. The world shimmered and reformed, the area they arrived in a dark, spacious tunnel with a pale glow at the end of it. Audrey pulled away from the woman. "Where are we?"

"Hush." The woman kept her voice low. "My magic isn't strong enough to take us far. We're in the tunnels that lead to the river." She took a step towards the glow. "This way. Before night falls and we can't see anything in here."

"I thought people could see in the dark if they had magic." She cautiously followed the woman, careful where she stepped. "What else goes down this tunnel?" She eyed the water that ran along the middle of the tunnel, glinting in the limited light.

"Not all can see in the dark and the bath and laundry water are tipped down some of the pipes to keep the tunnels regularly flowing."

"Is that all?" She tried to move further away from the water. "No other waste water?"

The woman shook her head. "They wouldn't want the tunnels to smell. It'd rise up and fill the mansion."

"Why do they have a dungeon in a mansion?" Audrey stared at the circle of light that grew larger at the end of the tunnel.

"Many places have somewhere to hold enemies."

Audrey stepped out of the tunnel, taking deep breaths of the fresh air. The sun had nearly set and cast a red-gold glow across the landscape. Night was coming. "What about the wolves?"

"We need to find somewhere safe." The woman hurried towards the river.

"What is in this direction?"

"The water will help mask our scent if they use hounds to track us." The woman waded into the water.

Audrey followed, gasping at the cold. "I never thanked you for helping me escape with Tanwen."

"She was always good to the humans who served her whenever she visited with her husband. I never served her, but listened to the ones who did talk about it. A pity the same can't be said for Gower." The woman remained in the water, staying close to the bank.

Audrey drew alongside her. "I'm Audrey."

The woman glanced at her. "Saffron." She continued to wade through the water. "Why did you set me free? Don't you have your own magic you could have used once you were free of the guard?"

"I have magic." She didn't know if she should tell Saffron that she couldn't use it. Not with how Merrick had reacted about letting people know about her fear of tight spaces. "Why would I leave you behind when you risked yourself to save us?"

"I saved Tanwen. Not you."

"It worked out that way all the same." She shivered, the light rapidly fading and the day growing cooler. "How long do we need to stay in the water?"

"Until it's time to get out."

Chapter Twenty-Eight

Audrey pressed her lips together rather than make one of the cutting replies that came to mind. Past the initial urge to comment, she drew in a deep breath, slowly releasing it. "Where are we going?"

"The Fringes. It's easy to become lost there," Saffron said.

"I don't doubt it." Audrey continued to wade through the water, frequently checking over her shoulder. "How far away is the Fringes?"

"We won't reach there until after dark."

"We what?" Audrey demanded.

Saffron glanced at her, not replying.

"We can't be in the forest after dark." She clearly remembered what it had been like to face the wolves. There were no sharpened saplings around here with which to fight them. Or anything else.

Again Saffron only glanced at her.

Audrey wanted to demand what they were going to do, but obviously the woman had said all she planned to say. She rubbed at her skin, wishing the cold water helped cool more than her feet. Frowning, she ran her hand over her arm again before placing her palm against her cheek. Her skin felt like it burned, a strange itch forming beneath the skin. She drew in a sharp breath, Merrick's words coming back to her. 'It's a burning need, like I have to use it or it will eat away at me. An itch that's impossible to scratch.' Fear raced through her. Would she end up with the same wild look in her eyes? Panic clawed at her, the magic feeling like it wanted to escape, burning through her skin in an effort to be used. She felt like she might explode with how it pressed against her skin.

The sensation reminded her of being in a confined space. Instead of pressing in on her it was pushing out from her and yet it felt like the same suffocating feeling. She wrapped her arms around herself, trying to ignore the sensation. It didn't help much. What did help was the sun setting and darkness settling around them, the evening cooling off with a slight breeze. The coolness against her skin eased the burning sensation and she was tempted to wade out to the middle of the river and sink beneath the water.

It wasn't until Saffron led her from the river that Audrey realised she could see in the dark. Not perfectly, the forest was still filled with shadows, but enough that she could see where she was going and not run into any trees. The sound of a wolf howling slowed her steps and she scanned the area. "What do we do if they find us?"

"Keep moving. It's a long way off." Saffron didn't slow. "If they come close we climb a tree."

"How will we know they're close?"

"You'll know."

She picked up her pace, keeping close to Saffron, the sound of wolves howling regularly breaking the silence of the night. The sound continued to grow closer as they trudged through the forest. Eventually, she frowned, realising it truly was silent. More silent than it had initially been.

Saffron stopped. "Find a tree."

Audrey stumbled, sidestepping so she didn't run into Saffron. "They're here?"

"They're close." Saffron headed for the nearest tree with widespread branches. "Choose a different tree so they aren't focused on the one tree."

She was barely several metres from the ground when a pack of wolves came rushing towards the two trees, circling them, snapping and snarling at the bases. She scurried further up, the wolves as large as the ones at the cottage had been. She clung to the trunk, the branch she sat on creaking when one of the wolves threw itself at the base of the tree. "What do we do now?"

"Wait for morning or for them to be distracted by different prey."

She wanted to argue that she wasn't prey. Staring at the snapping and snarling wolves below, she couldn't bring herself to say the words. She tried. Several times. It wasn't until she realised that she didn't believe the words and that it was now impossible to lie that she closed her eyes, pressing her forehead against the rough bark of the tree. They were going to die. The tree shuddered. Either they'd be shaken from the tree or one of Gower's people would track them down.

Anger rushed through her and it was all she could do to contain the magic that wanted to escape, burning at her under her skin, like acid eating away at her body. A rush of air beneath her feet had her peering at the ground in time to see a wolf leap for her. He missed, but he was too close for comfort.

Rising to her feet, she perched on the branch she'd been sitting on, reaching for the one above her. The tree shuddered again and there was a snap as the branch she held, broke. For a second she thought she'd managed to keep her balance. The tree shuddered again and she plummeted to the ground, a section of the branch in her hand, the rest having been broken off as she crashed past another branch.

She hit the ground hard, landing on her side, raising her hand with the section of the branch in an effort to protect herself from the wolves. A fresh, sweet scent filled the air, a metallic scent mixed with it. Magic rushed from her, knocking the wolves off their feet, giving her a chance to rise to hers. She clutched the piece of branch, swinging it back and forth like a club when one of the wolves gained its feet and came in for the attack. She backed away, feeling like her magic was about to escape again, the burning sensation gone.

"Climb a tree," Saffron called out.

Audrey didn't have time to move. Several wolves attacked at once. Her magic rose, knocking them back, the branch hitting the one the magic missed. Once more the magic escaped, knocking wolves from her. Darkness felt like it closed in on her, making it impossible to figure out what was going on. Everything was a blur and she kept moving, her branch swinging back and forth.

She had no idea how much time passed, but when

the darkness cleared, she realised Saffron shook her shoulder, warily watching her. "What happened?"

"You have iron sickness," Saffron said.

Audrey didn't bother correcting her. She caught sight of the branch she held, dropping it when she saw the blood staining it, backing away from the object. "What happened?" Was that how Merrick felt when his eyes had that wild look? And why had it hit her so bad the first time? Was it something to do with how damaged the magic had been that she'd gained? None of this had been in Madlen's journal. The Fae clearly had no idea what she was really doing.

"We need to keep moving." Saffron gestured in the direction they'd been travelling in. "Before the wolves return."

Audrey gave the branch a wide berth. "What did I do?"

Saffron was silent a moment. "Protected us." She took a step in the direction they needed to travel. "Are you ready to keep moving?"

She nodded even though she had no idea. Glimpses of images swirled through her head, none of them reassuring. "I attacked the wolves?"

"You protected us." Saffron strode through the trees, regularly glancing at Audrey.

She wanted to demand a better answer, but feared

what it might be. Remaining silent, she walked beside Saffron, trying not to think about the magic she'd used. It was slowly building again, the burning sensation increasing by the minute. "Do you know how to find the magic collector in the Fringes? I need to visit him."

Saffron didn't answer, only continued to walk towards the Fringes.

Audrey scanned the forest, the shadows feeling like they were filled with all kinds of creatures that might come after her. She kept telling herself there was nothing nearby and that nothing wanted to attack her, but she didn't believe a single thought and certainly wasn't able to voice any of them.

The wolves didn't start again until they could see the Fringes in the distance. Audrey turned to face the sounds, hands raised as if to fight them.

Saffron grabbed her arm. "We have to keep moving. They won't enter the Fringes."

Audrey shrugged her off. "They're too close. I'm not about to turn my back on them."

"They aren't. We have time to reach the Fringes." Saffron grabbed her arm again, tugging her towards the ramshackle town. "Hurry. Before they do come close."

She struggled with the need to remain and face

the wolves and the more sensible option of fleeing. The option she'd normally take. She shook her head, trying to clear it from the darkness that wanted to close in on her. Fear flared. She didn't want to lose time again. Didn't want to be left wondering what she'd done.

"Audrey." Saffron tugged on her arm.

She let the woman turn her in the direction of the Fringes, frequently glancing over her shoulder. They entered the town near a river, walking alongside it as they headed towards the magic collector's house.

Audrey's eyes narrowed when a Fae heading towards them walked too close. She veered towards him.

The Fae moved further away from the river, lowering their gaze.

"Audrey." Saffron tugged her towards the river. "He's not a threat."

She wanted to argue, but the words wouldn't form. Her lips curved into a smile as she realised why. "Of course he's not a threat. I could take him out." The words shook her. She'd never say anything like that. Not normally. She wanted to beg Saffron to tell her what was happening, but didn't trust her. Didn't trust anyone. She had a feeling that was the magic making her feel that way, but couldn't be certain.

Saffron led her to the magic collector's house, the lantern burning brightly by the front door. He answered on the first knock, looking them over.

"I need to get to Carralin Castle. I have magic you can take in exchange," Audrey said.

"Didn't I already organise a lift to the castle for you?" the magic collector asked.

"Yes and now I'm back and need another lift," Audrey snapped.

The magic collector started to close the door. "Come back when you have better control of yourself."

She placed her palm against the door, preventing him from closing it. "I am in control of myself and I need to return to Carralin Castle. Immediately."

The magic collector held out two small glass bottles. "Fill these."

She started to ask for a crystal when she realised only Saffron would be able to help her drain off the magic. She couldn't risk the woman ending up with some of her magic. Not after all she'd done to help. "How do I pull the magic out?" Surely she could use her magic a few more times before anything drastic happened. Look how many times Merrick had used his.

"Push it from you," Saffron said. "Push it into the palm of your hand."

She raised her hand, staring at her palm as she tried to follow the directions. She was about to say it was impossible when the magic pooled in her palm and she tipped it into the glass bottles, filling both of them. She fought against the darkness that wanted to close in on her, handing the bottles to the magic collector. "How do I get to Carralin Castle?"

"I'll get the details for you." The magic collector closed the door.

Chapter Twenty-Nine

Audrey waited for the magic collector to return, impatience arrowing through her. She wanted to get this over and done with. About to knock again, she lowered her hand when the door opened.

The magic collector held out a piece of paper. "There's a woman in the courtyard markets that's going past the castle tomorrow on the way elsewhere. The directions show you which shop she works at."

Audrey took the map, not bothering to look at it. "I need to go today, not tomorrow."

"Have you seen the time? It's nearly the middle of the night. She wants to leave around daybreak. Not long before she leaves. Go talk to her. She might be interested in leaving earlier." The magic collector tried to close the door.

Audrey glared at him. "You tricked me. I told you I needed to leave immediately."

The magic collector pushed against the door. "I've provided you with the next transport out of here." The door closed with a sharp sound.

Audrey banged on the door. "Open up. I haven't finished talking to you." She fought against the darkness. It didn't help that the magic burned under her skin. The brief respite from draining off some of it hadn't lasted long.

"Why don't we see if she's willing to leave sooner?" Saffron asked. "We can always come back to the doctor and see if he has another option for you."

"Doctor?" Audrey frowned. "What doctor?"

Saffron gestured towards the closed door. "The magic collector. He's a doctor."

Confusion washed over her, pushing the darkness further away. "Doctor." She said the word hesitantly, like it wasn't one she'd encountered before. Was this what Merrick felt every time he lost it? Fear swamped her and she backed away from the door. She couldn't lose herself again. An image of the bloodstained branch filled her mind and she struggled to push it aside.

Saffron tugged on her arm. "This way." She took the piece of paper from Audrey, examining it. "Not far from here. Come on. This way." She continued to tug on Audrey's arm.

They were nearly at their destination when two Fae came around a corner, grinning when they caught sight of them. One Fae reached for a sword while the other reached for a dagger. The dagger wielding one chuckled. "Two humans wandering about on their own. And one of them looks like she'd make the perfect pet for one of those wealthy nobles who love to spend their money on useless things."

Fear and anger exploded through Audrey, the darkness swamping her even though she tried to hold it at bay. She fought against it, trying to escape its clutches, other images breaking through. A fist connecting with skin, a dagger in her hand, blood. So much blood.

She came to her senses clutching a bloodstained dagger, dropping it when she realised what she held.

Saffron scooped it off the cobblestone street, holding it out to her. "You might need it again."

She backed away, shaking her head. "No." She frowned. "Where are we?"

"You chased them."

Her gaze was drawn to a stone and mortar wall, further along, recognising it. She nearly blurted out that she wanted to go home, but she kept the words to herself. She didn't trust anyone these days. Not that she knew if she could return home that way.

Could the portal be used from this end? Or would she end up somewhere else, completely lost? A shiver ran through her. She pretty much was lost, just not geographically.

"Are you ready to find your transport out of here?" Saffron asked.

"Mine? Aren't you coming too?"

Saffron shook her head. "There's no place for me at Carralin Castle. I have no people there."

Anger threatened to burst through her. She barely held it back. "There better be a place for you if you want it. Without your help, Tanwen wouldn't have been able to escape. Her or the baby."

Saffron took a step away, eyeing her cautiously. "You don't need to force them to take me in."

Her hands curled into fists and she held herself still, fighting against the darkness that wanted to close in on her. "Lead the way." The words were spoken through gritted teeth. When Saffron flinched, she wanted to reassure her. The words wouldn't come. They would have been a lie. She didn't trust herself so Saffron certainly shouldn't either.

Saffron frequently glanced at her, leading the way through the narrow streets and alleys. Reaching their destination, she stared at the ground, continuing to send glances at Audrey. "If you want to wait here, I'll see when she's ready to leave."

Audrey nodded, still struggling to maintain control. The place was too crowded and she kept expecting someone to attack. Even though she knew it was the magic making her feel paranoid, it didn't help. She couldn't get rid of the feeling that someone was out to get her.

Saffron returned from a different direction. "This way. I've organised food for us."

"Where did you come from?" Audrey looked from Saffron to the building she'd entered earlier.

"You were busy glaring at a group of Raptors when I came out so I found someone interested in buying the dagger and a place where we could afford to eat." Saffron took a step backwards. "Are you hungry?"

She started to say she had too many allergies to eat, then frowned. She was hungry and she'd been told the magic would make it possible to eat anything. It was probably past time to try. It didn't look like she'd be home any time soon. Following Saffron, she scanned the area, waiting to be attacked even though logically she knew that wasn't likely. In this crowd, the most that would happen was that someone would try to pick her pockets and learn they were empty.

Saffron led her to a noisy restaurant. Most of the tables were outside the building, along with most of the customers. A willowy Demi Fae with a green cast to her skin took their order and returned ten minutes later with plates of food.

Audrey eyed the pasta dish in front of her. It was filled with all the things she wouldn't normally be able to eat. Gluten, dairy and fructose along with a few other allergens. Taking a deep breath, in an effort to gather her courage, the smells filled her senses, making her mouth water. She had a mouthful, savouring the flavours. Another mouthful quickly followed and she cleaned her plate within minutes. She froze, fear beginning to rise, the darkness starting to close in on her. Nothing happened. The fear faded and she pushed away the darkness. A smile formed. She could eat what she wanted. The smile faded. But it meant avoiding iron. Rising to her feet, she glanced around the dining area. "Ready to go?"

Saffron finished up the last of her food, signalling the Demi Fae so she could pay for the meal.

Audrey slipped through the crowd, waiting out past the tables for Saffron. It was less crowded and she could see the enemy approaching. The thought shocked her and she focused on her parents and needing to return to them. It didn't help. That brought with it thoughts of Madlen and what she'd done to them. Her hands curled into fists.

"This way." Saffron hurried ahead of her, glancing over her shoulder to check that she followed.

Audrey strode after her, glad of the interruption. Her ability to think clearly was obviously gone. She glared at a Fae who came close, a sense of satisfaction washing over her when he scurried out of her way. She tried to push that feeling aside, but it remained.

Saffron spoke to the Fae who would give them a lift to the castle while Audrey glared at her, Saffron frequently looking in her direction. The journey to the castle was made in silence, Audrey eventually falling asleep to be regularly jarred awake by a rush of anger and the sensation of her magic trying to burn through her skin. It ate away at her, causing an itch she couldn't scratch and she found herself regularly rubbing at her arms, tempted to scratch away the skin to release the pressure. She maintained enough self-control not to do that, but it was close at times.

Reaching the castle, Audrey gave the Fae a nod, dragging Saffron away while she was thanking her for the lift, heading for the castle entrance. Two knights got in her way. "Where's Merrick?"

One of the knights glanced over his shoulder. "I'll send for him."

"Don't bother. Tell me where he is." She tried to step past them.

The knight stopped her, beckoning a servant forward. "You will wait here until Merrick is brought to you."

Her gaze arrowed in on the sword the knight had sheathed at his side, anger flaring.

Saffron grabbed hold of her arm, tugging her away from the knights. "Audrey. They're protecting the castle. It's their job."

"Protecting it from me?" Anger swirled through her, the darkness trying to close in on her.

Merrick ran towards her. "Audrey!"

Before she could move, she was enveloped in his arms and held tight. "Where's Luw?"

Merrick pulled slightly away from her, frowning. "Are you all right?"

She shook her head. "No. Now where is Luw?"

"What is the problem?" Merrick's gaze travelled over her. "Are you hurt?"

She pulled away from him. "Why won't you tell me where Luw is?"

Saffron lightly touched her on the arm. "Tell him. How can he know the importance if you don't tell him?"

Merrick looked from one to the other. "What is going on and who are you?"

Audrey gestured towards Saffron, struggling to keep a grip on her sanity. "She saved Tanwen's life. Gower had her in his dungeon. You owe her."

"You returned to Gower's? Are you insane?" Merrick demanded.

She jabbed a finger against his chest. "Do you seriously think I would have willingly returned there? Luw took me. Now where is he?"

"Luw?" Merrick frowned. "My knight Luw?"

"I don't know another Luw. Where is he?" She shouted the words at him, internally cringing at how she acted. She wanted to push all the magic from her. Wanted to return to being herself again. This wasn't her. Not in the slightest.

Merrick's jaw tightened. "He went with Tanwen to visit Siani." He formed an autumn leaf, the scent of his magic more metallic than that of baked apples.

Audrey grabbed hold of his arm. "You aren't leaving me behind." A small voice deep within her mind protested him using magic. The rest of her wanted to demand he take her to her brother.

The world shimmered and reformed. Tanwen yelled at Jordan and the knight, demanding why they hadn't done something. Spotting Audrey, Jordan tried to step around the Fae, who prevented him.

Audrey strode towards them. "Let my brother go." Her voice was low and menacing, a tone she'd never heard before.

"Audrey?" Jordan took a step back from her. "Is that you, Aude?"

Shock rushed through her, bringing with it a moment of sanity. "Barely." She glanced at the three in front of her. "What happened?"

"Luw took Siani," Jordan said. "Grabbed hold of her and vanished. Why would he take Siani?"

"He's Gower's son," Audrey said.

"What?" Merrick demanded. "When did you find that out?"

"When he kidnapped me," Audrey said.

"He kidnapped you?" Jordan asked.

"I need to go after Siani." The scent of Tanwen's magic filled the air.

"He'll kill the baby," Audrey said.

"What baby?" Merrick looked from Audrey to his sister. "What is going on?"

Tanwen rested a hand on her stomach. "I didn't know until after my husband died. I've been hiding it ever since with a glamour. Only Siani knew." Her stomach rounded, her garments also changing. "It's been getting difficult, but the attacks made me wary. It's why I wanted to go home to our parents. I planned to stay there the four months until the baby was born. I was going to tell all of you once I was safely at Carralin Castle." She paused a moment. "Things didn't work out."

Jordan stared at Tanwen's stomach. "How did you do that?"

"I'll go after her." Merrick formed an autumn leaf, the scent of his magic nearly completely metallic.

Chapter Thirty

Once again Audrey grabbed hold of Merrick, her gaze going to Tanwen. "Keep my brother safe."

Tanwen met her gaze, inclining her head. "Bring my daughter home."

Audrey barely had time to nod before the world shimmered and reformed. They were outside the mansion. She wanted to rush inside and find Siani. From the wild look in Merrick's eyes, he wanted to do the same. "No. You'll get her killed."

"Get who killed?" Merrick demanded.

Audrey drew in a shuddery breath, wrapping her arms around him. "It's hard to hold on, but you have to. Your niece needs you." She needed to find Luw. He couldn't be left free. He knew where she lived. "I know the room Tanwen was kept in. They might have put Siani there."

The wild look remained in his eyes, none of her words changing his expression.

"Merrick!" She tightened her arms around him, deciding to try a different tactic. "I know where he might be. I can picture the room clearly. Tell me how to use magic to travel there."

"Are you picturing it now?"

She brought an image of the room to her mind. "Yes."

Merrick's magic filled the air and the world shimmered and reformed as the room where Audrey and Tanwen had been imprisoned. He dragged out of her grip at the sight of Gower holding out parchment and a nib pen to Siani. He strode across the room towards them.

Audrey hurried after him, worried he'd get himself killed. But when Merrick drew his sword, Audrey threw herself out of the way, remembering last time. She collided with Siani, feeling the rush of air from the swing of the sword. The fight came closer and she dragged Siani against the wall, her gaze momentarily resting on the chains preventing the Fae from escaping.

"The guard at the door has the keys," Siani said.

Audrey looked at the two fighting then at the door. There was no way past them. Not without risking being struck by one of the swords. Once was more than enough.

"Audrey?" Siani tugged on the chains. "I can't get out of here. He wants me to sign over the castle or he'll kill me. But it won't matter in four months."

The words made her think of the unborn baby Tanwen had been hiding. She had no doubt that was what Siani referred to. Taking a deep breath, she momentarily closed her eyes, trying to ignore the burn from the magic that wanted to escape. That wanted to be used. She couldn't let that happen. She needed to be able to think clearly.

Gower's sword glanced off Merrick's, coming straight towards her. Without thinking, Audrey raised her hand, the magic rushing through her. Darkness swamped her. She didn't fight against it. There wasn't time. She caught glimpses. Like flashes of photographs. Forcing the sword away, wrenching the door open, someone screaming a familiar name, grabbing the sword from the startled guard, pushing him from her when he tried to attack, his body flying across the room to land beside Siani.

Another attacked from behind and she spun to face them. Again the images flashed past her. Luw with a sword, his face angry. Blood dripping down his face. Her standing over his body, confusion hitting her as she looked up to see Merrick stood over Gower, and Siani called their names.

She struggled to figure out what was going on, her gaze going between Merrick, who looked equally confused, and Siani who stood by the door, no longer chained.

Her gaze fell on the sword, blood dripping down the blade. Shock burst through her and she dropped the weapon, backing away from Luw. "I killed him?" The words were soft, fear filling them.

"He's alive." Siani took a step towards her. "Are you yourself again? Will you attack me?"

"I attacked you?"

Siani shrugged. "I shouldn't have come up behind you."

Merrick knelt at Gower's side, checking for a pulse. "He's dead. We need to go." He wiped his sword on Gower's clothes before sheathing it. Rising, he looked towards the door. "Why hasn't anyone come to see what is going on?"

Siani glanced over her shoulder. "They did. Gower sent them away. Said that he and Luw could manage a human and a barely grown Fae." She took another step into the room, clutching a ring of keys, and closed the door. "I doubt they knew what to think when the two of you became crazier and crazier."

Audrey stumbled towards Merrick, her body aching and some of the blood on her quite possibly her own. "How do you feel? You shouldn't have used your magic." Guilt struck her that she hadn't protested. All she'd thought about was her brother being in danger.

Merrick slipped an arm around her waist, drawing her close. "You shouldn't have used yours."

She looked up at him, tempted to argue. The words wouldn't come. Frustration arrowed through her. Not being able to lie was going to make life extremely difficult. Of course she should have used her magic, her brother was in danger. Her lips curved into a smile. Maybe it wouldn't be so bad after all. "You weren't about to leave your sister in danger so why should I have left my brother in danger?"

Merrick grinned, his expression immediately sobering. "I wouldn't leave you in danger either."

"The two of you can kiss and tell each other how much you care later. We have to get out of here." The scent of Siani's magic filled the air. "I'll bring someone back."

Merrick started towards her, not able to reach her before she vanished. "She doesn't always end up where she plans to go. She's still learning."

"Does it matter? Can't she keep trying until she gets it right?"

"If only it was that simple. She might end up somewhere dangerous."

Before Audrey could comment, a sound had her spinning in Luw's direction. He struggled to rise. She started towards the sword she'd dropped. There was no way she was going to let Luw have the chance to attack either of them.

Merrick tugged her back to his side, his gaze on the knight. "If I was you, I wouldn't move."

Luw dropped back against the floor with a groan, gingerly touching his head. "The castle should have gone to Gower."

"Your father," Merrick said.

Luw glanced at the body not far from him, remaining on the floor. "He promised I could inherit."

"The castle was never meant to be his. It has always gone to the oldest with the other siblings given smaller estates of their own. It would only have gone to Gower if there'd been no child," Merrick said.

Siani returned as Merrick spoke, Tanwen and a knight with her. "Signing it over to him wouldn't have been legal. It isn't mine to give away or sell. It always goes to the oldest child. And if the oldest child dies without an heir, it goes to their sibling. I have no choice in what happens to it."

"That can't be right," Luw said. "Gower told me it should have been his."

Tanwen looked down at Gower, no longer hiding her pregnancy. "And so it would have if he'd only been born ten minutes earlier." She turned to Luw. "Did he tell you he and his brother were twins?"

Luw stared at her stomach, now visible to him. "No."

"I'm certain there are a lot of things he never told you." She gestured the knight forward. "See that he's locked in our dungeon and notify my parents that Gower is dead. If they wish to take his estate they'd best move quickly before someone else realises."

The knight nodded, grabbing hold of Luw and vanishing.

Tanwen looked at each of them. "I can only take two and I can't leave Siani behind." She sent her daughter a look. "You shouldn't have followed. I told you to remain behind."

Audrey's gaze was drawn to Tanwen's stomach. "What about the baby? Is that counted as one of the ones you can take?"

Tanwen shook her head. "No. The baby is considered part of me."

"If we don't take Gower's body with us we have no chance of claiming the place." Siani grabbed Audrey's hand, tugging her away from Merrick. "I'll help."

The world shimmered and reformed. They were in a forest. Audrey looked around, not recognising the area. Beside her, Siani swore, a word Jordan often used and Audrey wondered what else her brother might have taught the Fae.

Siani's magic filled the air. "It works most of the time. Don't mention we didn't end up back in my room. No one has to know." The world shimmered and this time when it reformed, they were in Siani's room where her mother stood waiting.

"You were lost, weren't you," Tanwen said.

Before Siani had to answer, Audrey spoke. "Where's my brother? And my parents. Are all of them okay?"

Siani grabbed Audrey's hand again. "I'll show you where Jordan is. Or at least where we left him."

"Siani." Tanwen's voice was sharp.

Siani paused by the open door. "What?"

"Stay in the castle. I won't have you in danger during this."

Siani sighed. "Fine. I'll stay in the castle." She stepped out of the room, taking Audrey with her, continuing to hold her hand until they entered the room where Jordan was.

Audrey was tempted to sigh when she saw her mum was with him, giving him a lecture from his expression. "Why didn't you warn me?" She kept her voice low, her gaze darting to her mum to let Siani know what she meant.

"Is it a problem?" Siani kept her voice low too.

"I'm covered in blood. Of course it will be a problem." She started to turn away, wanting to escape before her mum noticed.

"Audrey!" Joan strode towards her. "What have you done to yourself?"

She took a step back. "I want to let you know I'm safe before I have a wash."

"Don't you dare go anywhere," Joan ordered.

Jordan grinned. "Looks like it's your turn for the lecture."

Chapter Thirty-One

Anger burst through Audrey and the darkness started to close in. She needed to get out of the room in a hurry. "I need a wash. The blood is starting to dry on me." Ignoring the shocked expression on her mum's face, she almost ran from the room. She didn't get far before she ran into Merrick.

He held onto her. "What's wrong? Did something happen?"

"I can't do this." She clung to him.

"Do what?"

"I don't want to hurt my family."

"What happened?" His arms tightened around her.

"It's like a darkness. Then I have no idea what I do or who I hurt. I thought I'd killed Luw. When I saw him lying at my feet and that I held a bloodstained sword, I really thought I'd killed him. I can feel it already. The magic trying to burn its way through me. Forcing me to use it."

Merrick kept one arm around her, cupping her face with his hand. "We'll face it together. I'll send everyone from my home and you and I will stay there together. We'll drain the magic off by using crystals and won't use our magic until it's back to normal."

"My magic has never been normal. What if it doesn't become normal?" The darkness pressed in on her and she struggled to keep it at bay. It didn't help that the magic burned her skin, making it as hot as his.

"We'll figure that out when we get to it."

"What about Madlen? Are we going to leave her to continue her experiments?"

"We can't do anything until it's safe to use our magic again, but I've got a feeling we won't be the only ones going after her. Idris sent a letter thanking us. His magic is already easing and he will go after her once it's back to normal. He asked if we were interested in joining him."

She tried to say 'no', but the word wouldn't form. Surely she didn't want to take on Madlen. That was crazy. "I don't know how to fight."

"I can teach you." His lips slowly curved into a

smile. "But from the bits I can remember, you did well for someone who doesn't know how to fight."

"That wasn't me."

"You might be surprised." He drew back from her. "I don't know about you, but I could do with a wash."

A wry smile formed. "That was where I was heading. Until I ran into you."

He chuckled. "You can run into me any time." Keeping an arm around her waist, he walked with her to her room, stopping a servant along the way to have them organise baths for the two of them. He stopped at her door, smiling at her. "I'll return after I've washed and bring a crystal and some bottles. We'll drain off our magic before we join everyone for dinner. I'm afraid it will only be your mother and brother and my niece. Everyone else is busy taking control of Gower's estate."

"Okay." She started to draw away from him.

He drew her close again, his lips meeting hers.

Returning his kiss, her arms slid around his neck, the drying blood on her momentarily forgotten. Eventually, she drew back, a noise in the hallway catching her attention. It was the servants with water for her bath. "You really need indoor plumbing."

Stepping back, Merrick chuckled. "I dare you to say that to my parents. They're a few hundred years old and very set in their ways." With a grin, he turned and strode away.

She stared after him, her mouth open. A few hundred years old? Was he serious? Slowly shaking her head, she stepped into the bedroom where her bath was being poured. He had to be serious. It was impossible to lie. Pushing aside the unsettling thought, she closed the door once the servants had left and had a bath, changing into the clothes they'd placed on the bed for her.

Dinner was full of arguments and Audrey was relieved they'd drained off most of their magic before going to the dining room. She thought of the seven bottles they'd filled between them, locked in a safe in Merrick's room. She shuddered at the thought of someone getting hold of the magic and what it might do to them.

"Are you paying attention to me, Audrey?" Joan demanded.

She tried not to sigh, but it escaped anyway. "I can't return home yet. I've already told you there are things I have to deal with here."

"Yet you won't tell me what those things are," Joan said.

"I'm not going back home either," Jordan said.

Joan pointed a finger at him. "You will do as you're

told and you're finishing school. This isn't our world. It's bad enough we'll have to spend the rest of our days eating their food." She looked pointedly at Audrey. "None of us should have accepted their magic."

Audrey pressed her lips tightly together. She hadn't exactly chosen to have magic. It had been an accident. But she wasn't about to tell her mum. She'd probably find a way to blame Merrick.

"Why not?" Jordan asked. "I'd accept magic if it was offered to me."

"Did you want magic?" Siani asked Jordan.

Joan interrupted before Jordan could answer. "No, he doesn't. We're not staying here."

"I am."

Hearing the familiar voice, Audrey turned in her seat to see Fred stood in the doorway, looking gaunt and fatigued. "Dad."

Jordan turned to Audrey. "See. I told you." He rose to his feet. "I'm staying here with Dad."

Her brother's words reminded her of Mick's prediction. Surely her parents weren't headed for a divorce.

"You weren't planning on discussing anything with me?" Joan also rose to her feet.

Audrey continued to eat, wanting to leave before another argument started.

"There's no way I can live in our world. Not with magic. Or at least not without problems." Fred glanced at Merrick. "I've been offered a job. They call accountants bookkeepers in the realms of the Fae so at least I have a skill that will be useful here."

"How can you want to stay after all that has happened to us?" Joan demanded.

Finished the rest of her food, Audrey placed her cutlery on her plate, trying not to grin when she noticed Jordan had moved closer to Siani who had a handful of magic. She should probably stop him, but it wasn't like she could talk since, like her dad, she had magic. At least if he had magic, then her brother could eat what he wanted without needing to regularly eat Fae food. Rising to her feet, she pushed her chair back under the table.

"Where are you going?" Joan demanded.

"It's been a long day." Audrey walked towards the doorway.

"You are not moving in with Merrick," Joan stated.

Fred remained in the doorway. "They're dating?"

Audrey stopped in front of her dad. "I can't return yet. I have things to do. Things Merrick will help me with."

Merrick joined her in the doorway. "I'll protect your daughter while she stays with me." He smiled, glancing at Audrey before he continued speaking. "Not that I think she needs anyone to take care of her. She's more than capable of taking care of herself." He glanced at each of them. "And all of you too." His gaze rested on Fred. "If you will excuse me."

Fred stepped out of the doorway.

Audrey hurried after Merrick, ignoring her mum's demands to come back. It had been a long day. She shied away from images of bloody weapons. All she wanted to do was sleep and not think about anything for at least eight hours. And in particular, she didn't want to dream. She dreaded to think what she might come up with after her recent fights.

Merrick slowed, slipping an arm around her when she came alongside him. "Do you still want to stay with me while our magic settles?"

She slid her arm around his waist. "Yeah."

"What about once our magic has settled?"

She looked up at him, studying his face. He looked both hopeful and worried. She wanted to give him an answer. "I don't know. Sorry, but I really don't know."

He smiled. "You can't lie."

She laughed softly. "Yeah. I've discovered that already."

"It's all right. We'll work it out along with our magic." He came to a stop at her door, turning to face her, keeping his arm around her. "We'll work it out together."

She thought about his words, returning his smile. "Yeah. Together." She rose onto the tip of her toes, her lips meeting his. They were broken apart by a noise and she turned to see her mum coming towards them. She wanted to beg him to stay. "You should probably go."

"Will you be fine?"

"Yeah. She's not about to hurt me."

"I wish I could form a leaf for you to call me if you should need me."

"Don't. Promise me you won't use your magic again. Not until it's right."

"Only if you'll promise the same."

"Yeah." She briefly kissed him, ignoring her mum impatiently waiting. When he left, she opened her door, leaving it open for her mum to follow her.

"I know we have you to thank for getting us out of this mess, but that doesn't mean you're capable of facing the dangers in this world," Joan said.

She examined her mum, seeing the fear in her eyes.

A fear she wasn't accustomed to seeing. She crossed the distance between them, hugging her mum before stepping back. "It's going to be okay. We're all going to be okay." Like Merrick had pointed out, she was capable of taking care of herself. And those she cared about. When she thought of who she cared about, Merrick was amongst their number.

"We won't be okay if we stay here," Joan said.

"They're in our world too. Returning home won't keep us away from them."

"That girl gave your brother magic. There has to be some way of undoing it."

Audrey shook her head. "No, there isn't."

"Why do you need to stay here?"

She didn't answer immediately. Really didn't want to risk her mum being more worried than she already was. "Madlen's experiments messed up my magic. I need to stay here until it's fixed."

"Your father seems fine."

Audrey doubted it, but shrugged instead of answering. She'd talk to him tomorrow and let him know what needed to be done to help him get his magic sorted. For now, she wanted to sleep. "I'll come home when my magic is sorted." That didn't mean she'd stay. She still had to figure that out.

"You will?" Joan asked.

Audrey grinned at the look of surprise on her mum's face. "Yeah. I will."

"You're not planning on staying here?"

She tried to think of a way to answer. This was certainly one of those times when not being able to lie was a nuisance. "Staying with Merrick was never about staying in the realms of the Fae. It was about fixing my magic before coming home."

Joan hugged her. "I'm so relieved."

Audrey returned the hug before drawing away. "I need sleep. I'm exhausted."

Joan nodded. "I'll see you in the morning."

Audrey managed to keep her expression neutral. Hopefully, morning wouldn't bring more demands. "Okay." She walked her mum to the door, standing with it half open as she watched her leave, tempted to go the next morning before anyone was awake.

Sighing, she closed the door and readied herself for bed. She'd faced Gower and Luw, not to mention stealing Madlen's journal pages. Surely she could face her mum the next morning. A wry smile formed. Facing Madlen, angry over her stolen pages, had to be the better option. Putting out the lamp, she climbed into bed, pulling the blankets up.

As exhausted as she was, she didn't instantly go to sleep. Thoughts of what the future would bring kept her awake. There were so many decisions she needed to make. Big decisions. Life changing decisions. She was still thinking about all of them when she sank into sleep.

Chapter Thirty-Two

Audrey changed out of her school uniform, taking an autumn leaf from the trinket container on her duchess. She raised it to her lips. "Merrick." The leaf was dragged from her fingers by an impossible breeze, the leaf slipping behind her curtain and out the closed window. She had no idea how it managed to do that, but over the past few months, she'd learned that magic had its own rules and way of doing things. Many of them contradicting the rules of her world.

Thinking of magic brought to mind the numerous bottles they'd filled during the two weeks it had taken their magic to become normal. Idris had also managed to cure himself from Madlen's experimentation and was currently looking for her. She'd disappeared, along with the nephew. She was sure that if anyone could find Madlen, it'd be Idris. He was obsessed with making her pay for all she'd done. Not that she blamed him.

Picking up her sword, she buckled it on, the scent of magic filling her room, a faint metallic scent mingling with one of baked apples. Her magic also had a slight metallic scent to it. Turning, she smiled at Merrick, going into his arms. "What took you so long?"

He kissed her first, drawing back slightly to smile at her. "Demands? Is that how you greet me?"

"Yep. Now what took you so long?"

He formed an autumn leaf and gave it to her. "I had a visitor."

Drawing away from him, she put the leaf in her trinket container along with the other ones in there. She smiled at the sight of them. He liked to make sure she always had plenty of them in case she needed to contact him. She'd done the same for him, giving him several of the pale green leaves she was able to form with her magic. "Who?" She faced him again.

"Idris. It seems he's discovered where Madlen has been hiding." He tugged her back to him. "Want to go after her with us?"

A grin formed. "That's good timing." The June-July holidays had started today and she'd planned to spend them in the realms of the Fae visiting her dad and brother. Her mum had argued against it, but she'd refused to give in. Siani had also invited her to visit her castle. Her and her mother had taken Saffron there with them. She supposed she could visit next school holidays. "Think we can deal with her in two weeks? Or less since time doesn't pass the same."

"She's hiding in your world and not doing too well from what Idris has learned. Iron sickness."

She met his gaze, not sure if she should bring up something that had been bothering her. "It did something to us, her experiment, didn't it."

"Yes. We seem to be less susceptible to iron sickness."

"Do you think she knows she figured out a cure for iron sickness. Or at least a partial cure."

"No. And she never will with her current methods."

"I'm glad. Who knows what she'd do with the knowledge if she did."

"I'm not about to tell her and neither is Idris. And your father has no plans to return to this realm so he'll never figure it out. We're the only ones who've survived her experiments."

She thought of the ones they'd rescued. The ones who hadn't been given any magic. None of their partners had survived. When someone had gone back to the house in the realms of the Fae, they'd been too far gone, dead within days. Some of the ones from Madlen's basement had chosen to remain in the realms of the Fae while the rest had returned to their own world. "Do you think she's been experimenting on others since she disappeared?"

"I think she's been too busy hiding to do anything else."

"Good." She glanced at the bedroom door. "Mum is expecting us to join her for dinner before we go."

A pained expression momentarily crossed Merrick's face. "Are you sure that is necessary?"

Audrey laughed. Merrick mostly tried to visit her while her mum was visiting Fred and Jordan in the realms of the Fae, which was the first half of each week. She only worked half a week, her boss willing to reduce her hours since he and everyone else believed they'd lost Fred and Jordan during the abduction. They'd thought it best. Merrick had also told them of a fruit that could break Joan's dependence on Fae food, but it was near impossible to get.

Audrey tugged Merrick towards the door. "Yeah, it is necessary to join my mum for dinner." She paused a moment. "Where will we stay while we're chasing Madlen down in this world?"

"She's down south so it won't be here."

She laughed again, tempted to tease him about how relieved he must be. "Where is Idris?"

"The Fringes. We'll call him when we're ready."

"So we won't be returning to the realms of the Fae?" She rested her hand on the doorknob, leaving the door closed.

"Not yet. Once we've caught her. Did you have other plans?"

She shrugged. "Not really. I did want to see Dad and Jordan, but there were no set plans. I'd rather go after Madlen and make sure she can't experiment on anyone else again."

"Even if we didn't join him, Idris would make sure of that."

She looked into his eyes, seeing the excitement in them. A similar feeling stirred in her. She might actually get to use the sword skills Merrick had been teaching her.

Merrick chuckled. "You're looking forward to it too."

She grinned. "Yeah, I guess I am." She'd figured out a lot of things during the past few months. She liked living between both her world and the realms of the Fae and wasn't interested in giving either up. Magic was useful even with always needing to tell the truth. And she was willing to fight to protect those she cared about. All of those she cared about. She opened the door. "Come on. Before my mum is in here demanding what's taking us so long."

They strode to the table, greeting Joan who was already seated.

"No weapons at the table. How many times do I need to tell you?" Joan asked.

Audrey grinned at Merrick when he did the same as her and used his magic to hide that he wore a weapon.

"I know they're there," Joan said.

"We could have sent them somewhere else," Audrey said.

"Did you?" Joan asked.

Audrey sat at the table, smiling. "Anything is possible with magic." Her smile widened and she met Merrick's gaze when he sat across from her. Anything was possible and she was about to spend the next two weeks discovering exactly what was possible and what she was capable of. Madlen would regret coming after her family. Her hand rested on the hilt of her sword that remained invisible. So would the nephew and anyone else who harmed those she cared about. Like Idris, she'd hunt Madlen down until she was no longer a threat.

And when the end of the year came and she was no longer at school, who knew what she'd do next. Whatever it was, it wouldn't be ordinary and it probably wouldn't be safe. She continued to meet Merrick's gaze. And they'd do it together. Side by side, protecting each other, no matter the situation they ended up in.

Free Ebook

Subscribe to Avril's newsletter and receive a free ebook. This ebook is exclusive to those on her mailing list. To find out more about this offer visit:

www.avrilsabine.com/free-ebook

*

We value your privacy and will not sell, rent, exchange or loan your email address to third parties. Your information is confidential and you are under no obligation to remain on the mailing list and can unsubscribe at any time.

Acknowledgements

As well as many thanks to the usual crew, thank you to Emily for suggesting carnations and helping me describe them. And of course thanks to Adam for… well, for being Adam.

To The Reader

If you enjoyed this book, why not consider leaving a review to help other readers discover it too? Reader engagement is one of the few ways that lets an author know readers want more books in a particular series or genre. So leave a review and tell friends, not only about this book but also about other ones you've enjoyed, so you can continue to enjoy books by your favourite authors for years to come.

Dreams are meant to be lived,

Avril.

About The Author

Avril is an Australian author who lives with her family on acreage in South East Queensland. She writes mostly young adult and children's speculative fiction, but has been known to dabble in other genres. You can find more information about her at www.avrilsabine.com where you can also subscribe to her newsletter to be kept informed about new releases, current projects, blog posts and exclusive news.

Titles By Avril Sabine

Stories about strong characters and characters who discover their strengths.

Dragon Blood- Young Adult Urban Fantasy (with elements of romance)

(5 book series)

Book 1: Pliethin

Book 2: Wyvern

Book 3: Surety

Book 4: Knight

Book 5: Mage

Dragon Mage- Young Adult Urban Fantasy (with elements of romance)

(Series two of Dragon Blood series)

Book 1: Promise

Dragon Blood Chronicles- Young Adult Urban Fantasy (with elements of romance)

(Companion stand alone series to Dragon Blood)

Book 1: Oath

Book 2: Betrayed

Guardians Of The Round Table- Young Adult Fantasy LitRPG

(Co-written with Storm and Rhys Petersen)

Book 1: Dexterity Fail

Book 2: Goblin Boots

Book 3: Singed Feathers

Book 4: Frog Mage

Book 5: Crystal Mine

Book 6: Cursed Harp

Rosie's Rangers- Young Adult Western Steampunk

(6 book series)

Book 1: Justice

Book 2: Vengeance

Book 3: Treachery

Book 4: Accused

Book 5: Wanted

Book 6: Corruption

Mark Of Kings- Children's Fantasy

(Upper middle grade/preteen)

(4 book series)

Book 1: The Arena

Book 2: The Island

Book 3: The Assassin

Book 4: The King

STAND ALONE SERIES

Demon Hunters- Young Adult Urban Fantasy/ Horror (with elements of romance)

Book 1: Blood Sacrifice

Book 2: Retribution

Book 3: Tainted

Book 4: Premonition

Book 5: Cursed

Book 6: Feud

Book 7: Extrication

Plea Of The Damned- Young Adult Urban Fantasy/Paranormal

(6 book series)

Book 1: Forgive Me Lucy

Book 2: Forgive Me Aiden

Book 3: Forgive Me Jena

Book 4: Forgive Me Kobe

Book 5: Forgive Me Marti

Book 6: Forgive Me Dawson

Realms Of The Fae- Young Adult Urban Fantasy (with elements of romance)

The Sword (short story in Like A Girl Anthology)

Heart Of Stone

Book 1: A Debt Owed

Book 2: Marked By The Hunt

Book 3: The Magic Collector

Book 4: An Unexpected Betrayal

Book 5: Imprisoned By Iron

Fairytales Retold (Short Stories)

Snow-White And Rose-Red

The Twelve Brothers

The Light Princess

Beauty And The Beast

Sleeping Beauty

Aschenputtel

The Golden Bird

The Frog Prince

The Death Of Koshchei The Deathless

Myths And Legends Retold (Short Stories)

Ion, Son Of Apollo

Sir Gawain And The Maid With The Narrow Sleeves

Princess Ilse, The Giant's Daughter

YOUNG ADULT NOVELS

Young Adult Fantasy (with elements of romance)

Elf Sight

Earth Bound

Young Adult Urban Fantasy

Stone Warrior (with elements of romance)

The Jungle Inside

Young Adult Contemporary (with elements of romance)

Through Your Eyes

The Ugly Stepsister

Perfect Little Princess

Young Adult Contemporary/Paranormal

Whispers In The Dark (with elements of romance and same sex relationships)

Over Too Soon (with elements of romance)

Young Adult Sci-Fi

Experiment X-One-Six (Urban Sci-Fi/Superheroes)

An Endless Dawn (Post Apocalyptic Sci-Fi)

CHILDREN'S BOOKS

Dragon Lord (Preteen/early teens) (Fantasy)

The Irish Wizard (Upper middle grade) (Urban
Fantasy)

SHORT STORIES

Urban Fantasy

Eternally Late

Dealings With Joe

Glimpses (short story in That Moment When
Anthology)

Contemporary

The Brat Next Door

Fantasy LitRPG

(Set in the same world as Guardians Of The Round
Table Series)

Tales Of Inadon 1: The Disc (Co-written with
Storm and Rhys Petersen) (short story in Game On!
Anthology)

Post Apocalyptic Sci-Fi

Compulsive Directive

NONFICTION

A Year Of Weekly Writing Exercises (Creative Writing)

Cooking For Families With Allergies (Cooking) (Co-written with Storm Petersen)

Tell Me A Story, Grandma (Memoir)

For the most up to date details on available titles visit:

www.avrilsabine.com/books/bibliography

Realms Of The Fae Series

To learn more about this series visit:

www.avrilsabine.com/series/rotf

BOOKS AVAILABLE IN THE REALMS OF THE FAE SERIES

The Sword (short story in Like A Girl Anthology)

Heart Of Stone

Book 1: A Debt Owed

Book 2: Marked By The Hunt

Book 3: The Magic Collector

Book 4: An Unexpected Betrayal

Book 5: Imprisoned By Iron

Disclaimer

This is a work of fiction. Names, characters, businesses, places, events and incidents are either the products of the author's imagination or used in a fictitious manner. Any resemblance to actual persons, living or dead, or actual events is purely coincidental. The opinions expressed or beliefs held are those of the characters and should not be assumed to be the opinions or beliefs of the author.